CW00709183

'Why didn't you keep in touch, Fiona?'

'Aren't you forgetting something, Paul? It was you who left, you who went away.'

He stared at her in silence, then gently he said, 'I'm quite aware of that, and I thought you understood my reasons.'

She allowed herself a short laugh. 'Oh, yes, I remember—your career. You told me you had to go to further your career, that you didn't want a serious relationship. That was right, wasn't it?'

He frowned. 'Well, yes, basically I suppose that was right, but I didn't think you would have wanted it to be so final. I thought under the circumstances we would have at least remained friends.'

'And what circumstances were those?'

He continued to stare at her, as if he was unable to believe the attitude she was taking, then said, 'Fiona, I always believed that what we had was very special. Can you look at me and tell me I was wrong? Can you?'

Laura MacDonald is the pseudonym of the author, who lives in the Isle of Wight. She is married and has a grown-up family. She has enjoyed writing fiction since she was a child, but for several years she has worked for members of the medical profession both in pharmacy and in general practice. Her daughter is a nurse and has also helped with research for Medical Romances.

Previous Titles

ISLAND PARTNER
AN UNEXPECTED AFFAIR

ALWAYS ON MY MIND

BY

LAURA MacDONALD

All rights reserved including the right of reproduction in whole or in part in any form. This edition is published by arrangement with Harlequin Enterprises B.V. The text of this publication or any part thereof may not be reproduced or transmitted in any form or by any means, electronic or mechanical, including photocopying, recording, storage in an information retrieval system, or otherwise, without the written permission of the publisher.

All the characters in this book have no existence outside the imagination of the author, and have no relation whatsoever to anyone bearing the same name or names. They are not even distantly inspired by any individual known or unknown to the author, and all the incidents are pure invention.

First published in Great Britain 1997
by Mills & Boon Limited

© Laura MacDonald 1997

ISBN 0 263 77315 2

MILLS & BOON LIMITED
ETON HOUSE   18–24 PARADISE ROAD
RICHMOND   SURREY   TW9 1SR

All the characters in this book have no existence outside
the imagination of the Author, and have no relation
whatsoever to anyone bearing the same name or names.
They are not even distantly inspired by any individual
known or unknown to the Author, and all the incidents
are pure invention.

All Rights Reserved. The text of this publication or any
part thereof may not be reproduced or transmitted in
any form or by any means, electronic or mechanical,
including photocopying, recording, storage in an
information retrieval system, or otherwise, without the
written permission of the publisher.

This book is sold subject to the condition that it shall
not, by way of trade or otherwise, be lent, resold, hired
out or otherwise circulated without the prior consent of
the publisher in any form of binding or cover other than
that in which it is published and without a similar
condition including this condition being imposed on the
subsequent purchaser.

First published in Great Britain 1991
by Mills & Boon Limited

© Laura MacDonald 1991

Australian copyright 1991
Philippine copyright 1991
This edition 1991

ISBN 0 263 77315 9

Set in 10½ on 12 pt Linotron Palatino
03-9107-47206
Typeset in Great Britain by Centracet, Cambridge
Made and printed in Great Britain

CHAPTER ONE

STAFF NURSE Fiona Norris glanced round her tidy ward, noting with satisfaction the rows of neatly made beds and the eager expressions on most of the patients' faces as they awaited their visitors. Another quick glance, this time at the fob watch on the front of her uniform, showed that she had only another half-hour before her shift ended. If she was lucky she would have time to go to the supermarket before it closed. Her son Dominic was bringing a friend home to tea and Fiona wanted to collect some of their favourite crisps.

At the sudden sound of the telephone ringing in Sister's office Fiona moved swiftly across the ward, aware of the eyes of the patients on her. With her blonde hair neatly cut into a fashionable bob and secured under her white cap and the slimness of her figure accentuated by her blue belt, she cheered the heart of many a patient on the ortho-paedic unit of St Catherine's Hospital.

It was the consultant's secretary on the tele-phone, informing Fiona that Mr Rossington was bringing his new orthopaedic registrar to have a look round before he took up his position on the unit the following day.

Fiona sighed as she replaced the receiver. It looked as if she wouldn't be finishing on time after all. Normally it would have been Sister's job to receive the new registrar, but as Sister Jenkins was on leave and Sister Buchanan was sick, Fiona had been acting as ward sister, and the responsibility would automatically fall to her. Much as she had wanted to get away on time she would in no way shirk her duty. Recently she had applied for the post of ward sister, which would be coming vacant when Sister Jenkins retired, and she knew she was being considered for the position, just as she was fully aware of the fact that Marilyn Hughes, another staff nurse on the unit, had also applied and was being considered.

A quick look in the mirror above Sister's desk revealed that her cap was slightly askew, and she adjusted it carefully, at the same time checking her hair and regretting that her nose looked shiny. But there was no time to repair her make-up, for at that moment she heard the sound of footsteps in the corridor.

Fiona smoothed down her uniform and, straightening her shoulders, stepped out of the office.

Afterwards she was never certain of the exact sequence of events that followed; she only knew that somehow a group of visitors arrived at the exact time as Mr Rossington and the new registrar, that old Mrs Barnes, who'd had a total hip replacement, chose that moment to fall out of bed, and, to a cacophony of ringing bells and frantic cries for the nurse, she found herself staring up into the eyes of a man she hadn't seen for nearly seven years. A man she had thought she would never see again.

At the time it was as if Fiona was paralysed, rendered incapable of either movement or speech, as she gazed dumbly at Paul Sheldon. Then somehow her professional instincts took over as the commotion in the ward behind her penetrated her brain.

Vaguely she remembered going to the assistance of two of the other nurses on duty, one of whom, Jill Markham, a state-enrolled nurse, was her friend. Between them they lifted Mrs Barnes back into bed, whisking the curtains around her, shielding her from curious eyes before attempting to calm her down. Dimly Fiona recalled checking the old lady's pulse and blood-pressure before mechanically dialling for the duty houseman to come and examine her and if necessary prescribe analgesics or a sedative. And all the while her stomach churned as Paul Sheldon patiently waited in Sister's office with Mr Rossington for the crisis to be brought under control.

As she emerged from Mrs Barnes's cubicle Fiona glanced round at her once-tidy ward. The excitement had disrupted the other patients, who were all anxious to relate what had happened to their visitors, who by this time were crowding into the ward, some complaining that it was well past the time. But all this only half registered, for as Fiona made her way down the ward and back to the office the questions were crowding her mind.

What was he doing here? The medical secretary

had said her boss was bringing the new registrar down, but surely that couldn't be Paul Sheldon? Oh, dear God, no! prayed Fiona silently. You surely couldn't be that cruel! Not him of all people, and not only here at St Catherine's, but on this very unit!

He was standing with his back to the door, staring out of the window, as Fiona came into the office. Mr Rossington was seated at Sister's desk, looking through some papers in a folder. He looked up as Fiona came in.

'Ah, Staff Nurse Norris,' he said smoothly. 'Obviously we've chosen a bad moment.'

'Not at all, Mr Rossington,' replied Fiona as evenly as she could.

'I trust everything is now under control?' He raised bushy grey eyebrows.

'Of course,' she said, silently sending up a prayer of thanks that Mrs Barnes wasn't his patient.

'I've brought Dr Paul Sheldon to meet you. We're extremely fortunate that Dr Sheldon is joining us in Orthopaedics.' He half turned towards the figure at the window. 'Paul, this is Staff Nurse Fiona Morris. At the moment she's acting sister in charge, and we hope that before very long she'll receive her new grading.'

Paul Sheldon turned, and immediately his eyes met hers she felt her heart jolt uncomfortably against her ribs.

He had hardly changed at all, she thought with a pang as she stared helplessly at him. There was no hint of grey in the still thick dark blond hair, and the eyes that were neither blue nor grey still had the glint of amusement in their depths that she remembered so well.

Vaguely she was aware that Mr Rossington was still talking, but she had no idea what he was saying. Then, although Paul still held her gaze, he inclined his head in the consultant's direction.

'It's all right, Henry,' he said. And the voice was the same; the one that had remained in her head for seven long years. 'Staff Nurse Norris and I have already met.'

A surprised silence followed his words as Mr Rossington, interrupted in mid-sentence, looked from one to the other in sudden surprise. 'Really?' he said, then added breezily, 'Well, how fortunate; especially as you'll be working together so closely.' He gave a short laugh, seemingly oblivious or maybe simply baffled by the apparent tension in the small office.

In the end it was the sound of his bleeper that broke the tension, and Fiona indicated for him to answer it on the office telephone.

They remained silent as he took the call, with Fiona totally unable to look in Paul's direction, then Mr Rossington replaced the receiver and glanced at his watch, saying, 'I'm afraid I have to go—I'm needed in Theatre.'

Fiona gave an inward sigh of relief. All she wanted was to be alone to come to terms with the shock of seeing Paul Sheldon again. Her hopes were dashed a moment later, however, as Paul said smoothly, 'You carry on, Henry. I should like to stay, if Staff Nurse has the time to show me the ward.'

Fiona stiffened, not answering immediately. She would have given anything to refuse, anything not to have to show him around and answer the inevitable questions that would follow as soon as they were alone. Then, suddenly conscious of Mr Rossington's enquiring frown, she said quickly, 'Of course.' As the consultant stood up and moved towards the door, she followed him, saying rapidly, 'If you'd like to come this way, Dr Sheldon.'

Giving him no chance to say anything further and no opportunity to be alone with her in the office, she led him out into the ward.

Mr Rossington disappeared down the corridor and Fiona began to show Paul Sheldon around. They began in the female section, inspected the private cubicles, the sluice, the offices and store and finally the nurses' station, where Fiona introduced him to Jill Markham and Betty Stevens, a care assistant, who had just returned from her tea break, and then to Marilyn Hughes. She couldn't help noticing the speculative gleam in Marilyn's eye as she assessed the new registrar. Then they moved to the male part of the ward, repeating the whole procedure, finally ending up in the day-room, where some of the more mobile patients were watching television or entertaining their visitors.

Several smiled and waved to Fiona, and, while she responded as naturally as she could, she was very aware of the fact that her hands had grown clammy and that, throughout the entire time it had taken to familiarise the registrar with his new domain, she had not once looked at him. She had, however, been acutely aware of his presence at her side and had known that on more than one occasion he had been closely studying her.

By the time she had escorted him back to the office her hands were shaking. Leaving the door open, she walked to the desk, then turned to face him, hoping that he would now simply go, but when he walked right into the office and closed the door behind him, she knew it wasn't going to be that easy.

Desperately she wiped her damp palms down the sides of her uniform.

'What's wrong, Fiona?' he asked, trying to force her to look at him.

'What do you mean?' She gave a nervous little laugh.

'Well, you don't seem exactly pleased to see me.'

She took a deep breath. 'It's been a very long time, Paul, and it was a shock seeing you, that's all.'

'I agree, it has been a long time, and yes, it was a shock, but for me it was a very pleasant shock. . . You, however, don't seem quite so pleased. . .'

'Look, Paul, I'm sorry, but things are very different now. . .' She trailed off helplessly.

He laughed. 'I certainly wasn't expecting things to be the same after. . .how long is it? Six years?'

'Seven,' she said sharply, then, as he raised his

eyebrows in surprise, she added swiftly, 'What I mean is, it must be nearly seven years.'

He nodded and smiled as if remembering, and his eyes crinkled at the corners. Fiona felt her mouth go dry. If only he had changed in some way things might be easier. . .but, apart from the fact that he had filled out a little and seemed more mature, everything about him seemed to be just as she remembered, or rather just as she had spent the last seven years desperately trying to forget.

'Yes, it must be,' he mused. 'And I know a lot of water has flowed under the bridge since then. Don't worry, Fiona, I won't try to rake up anything you'd rather forget, but you have to admit that what we had was pretty special, wasn't it?' Again the amused gleam came into his eyes.

She stared at him speechlessly. How could he? How dare he say such things to her?

He seemed to misinterpret her silence and continued, apparently oblivious to her teeming emotions, 'I dare say by now you're happily married with a couple of kids. . .come on, tell me, I'm right, aren't I?'

Fiona shook her head. 'No. . .no, I'm not married.'

'Really?' Again the eyebrows raised in surprise. 'I quite thought someone would have snapped you up by now.'

She shook her head again and, turning away from him, picked up some temperature charts from the desk in a supreme effort to pull herself together.

'How long have you been at St Catherine's?' he persisted.

'Two years.' She kept her reply brief in the hope that he would give up questioning her, but her evasiveness only seemed to fuel his curiosity.

'And you've applied for ward sister?'

She nodded.

'Did you come straight here from Birmingham?' Paul's questions sounded casual, but Fiona knew him well enough to know he was probing now, and somehow she had to get him off the subject of her past. She was saved by a sudden tap at the door and, without even a glance at Paul, she called, 'Come in.'

When the door opened an anxious-faced woman stood there. 'Oh, Nurse, I'm sorry to bother you, but it's about my husband,' she said. 'He still seems to be in a lot of pain and I'm worried about him.' As she spoke she was joined in the doorway by a younger woman who, from the likeness, Fiona guessed to be the woman's daughter. She, however, seemed more forthright.

'We really need to know more about what my father's actually had done. No one's told us anything. . .'

Fiona took a deep breath, partly of relief. 'Perhaps you'd like to come in and we can have a chat. It's Mrs Evans, isn't it?' She indicated for the two women to come into the office, then turned and, opening the filing-cabinet, took out Mr Evans's file. It was the second day of his post-operative care after a laminectomy and spinal fusion, and it was understandable that his family were concerned.

As she opened the file, Paul spoke. 'I'll be on my way, Staff Nurse. Are you on duty tomorrow morning?'

'Yes, Dr Sheldon.'

'In that case, I'll see you on ward round.' With a courteous nod to the two ladies, he left the room, and for a split second Fiona leaned against the filing-cabinet, weak with relief, before turning to invite Mrs Evans and her daughter to sit down.

Her relief was short-lived, however, as Mrs Evans inadvertently reminded her of what was to come. She watched Paul leave the room, then asked, 'Was that the surgeon who did my husband's operation, Nurse?'

Fiona shook her head. 'No, Mr Rossington did your husband's operation. That was Dr Sheldon.'

'Is he a surgeon?' asked the younger woman, and there was an unmistakable note of admiration in her voice.

'He's the surgical registrar—that means he'll be assisting the surgeons here,' Fiona explained.

'Oh, is he new, then?'

Fiona nodded. 'Yes, he's new, in fact he starts tomorrow,' she added, and her heart gave a sickening lurch as the full implication of Paul Sheldon's new position at St Catherine's finally hit her.

When at last her shift was over Fiona left the hospital, hurried to the supermarket and collected her shopping. Then, turning up the collar of her raincoat against the keen March wind, she headed for the tiny terraced house in the shadow of Merstonbury Cathedral where she lived with her mother and her son.

The daffodils were in full bloom in the square in front of the Cathedral, great masses of waving golden trumpets bringing all the promise of a warm spring in spite of the chill of the wind. The month had started quietly enough, but, like the proverbial lion, it was roaring its way into April.

It had been spring when Fiona had first met Paul Sheldon all those years ago. The daffodils had been out then too along the river-bank, she recalled. She had been with a party of student nurses enjoying an afternoon off, sitting by the river in the unexpected sunshine, while he had been with a crowd of medical students who had hired two punts to take down the river. They had waved and shouted to the girls, manoeuvring the punts close to the bank and encouraging them to join them.

Maybe it would have been better if she'd refused, Fiona thought grimly as she turned and passed under a stone archway into a cobblestoned square at the side of the great Cathedral, because if she had, she might never have met him, less still grown to love him. From the moment she had taken Paul Sheldon's outstretched hand, looked down into those eyes that were neither grey nor blue, those eyes that held a perpetual glint of amusement in their depths, and had then stepped into the punt, life for Fiona had never been quite the same again.

And now he was back, and she had no idea how she was going to cope.

She stopped outside one of the houses of mellow old stonework that centuries before had been almshouses and fitted her key into the lock. As the door swung open, she called wearily, 'Hello, I'm home.'

The house seemed unnaturally quiet, and, unbuttoning her raincoat, she stepped towards the stairs and called again, louder this time.

'Is that you, darling? I'm up here!' It was her mother's voice that replied, and, because it sounded so faint, Fiona knew she must be in the attic. She took her shopping through to the kitchen, filled the kettle and switched it on, then went back into the hall and climbed the stairs.

As she reached the landing she could hear muffled giggles and thumps coming from her son's room, where Dominic was obviously engaged in some adventure with his best friend, Neil. She smiled to herself and, deciding to leave them to play for a little longer, climbed the second set of stairs to the attic.

Fiona's mother, Lilli, was an artist, and when they had moved to Merstonbury they had converted the attic into a studio for her. She was a vague, dreamy sort of woman in her early fifties, petite and small-boned, with her wispy blonde hair caught back into an untidy knot. The most obvious likeness to her daughter was the green eyes, which lit up as she turned from her easel to greet Fiona. She was untidily dressed in an old pair of faded denims and a navy blue smock smeared with a veritable rainbow of oil paints. There was a smudge of vermilion paint on her cheek and wisps of hair had escaped from the knot, but somehow, in the way she held herself, or in the turn of her finely boned features, she achieved a look of elegance and chic that Fiona envied.

'Hello, darling.' She frowned. 'Is it that time already? I only came up to finish this one little bit and I got quite carried away. Are you early?'

Fiona smiled and looked at the easel, where a canvas was nearing completion. 'No, as a matter of fact I'm late, if anything.'

Lilli stared at her. 'Are you? Oh, my God, the boys. . .are they all right?'

'Yes, I'm sure they are—stop worrying! I heard them giggling when I came up the stairs, so they must be OK.'

'Well, it's not good enough.' Lilli began cleaning her brushes. 'I'm supposed to be looking after them, for heaven's sake! I told Neil's mother I'd keep an eye on them until you came home, but I tell you, I just got carried away. . .' She stared up helplessly at Fiona.

'You do more than enough as it is,' replied Fiona with a sigh. 'God knows what I'd do without you. . . I'd fully intended being early tonight, especially with Neil being here, but—well, something cropped up and I couldn't get away.' She had intended telling her mother about Paul Sheldon's new post at the hospital, but suddenly she found she couldn't put it into words.

'Talking of getting away, Fe, darling,' said Lilli suddenly as if something had just occurred to her, 'do you think you could get away tomorrow?'

'Tomorrow?' Fiona had been about to climb down the stairs again, but she paused with one hand on the rail and stared at her mother.

'Yes. The school rang—they've re-scheduled the parents' open day. Miss Simms would like you to go in the morning to discuss Dominic's work.'

'In the morning?' Fiona stared at her in dismay. 'What time?'

'Ten o'clock, I think she said,' Lilli replied vaguely.

'Ten o'clock? Oh, no, I couldn't possibly get away then.'

'Couldn't you swap a shift with someone?' Lilli asked hopefully, knowing that Fiona had done this sometimes in the past when something had cropped up unexpectedly.

Fiona slowly shook her head. 'No, I'm afraid that's out of the question tomorrow. I'm acting sister and we have our new registrar starting. If I don't go, Marilyn will do it, and I can't let that happen—it wouldn't look very good for me at all.'

'Oh, what a shame! Dominic so wanted you to go; he wants to show you the collage he's been working on, but never mind, it can't be helped.'

'Would you be able to go, Lilli?' asked Fiona hopefully. She had called her mother by her Christian name since she was a little girl, just as everyone did who knew her.

Lilli smiled and wiped the turps from her hands

down the front of her smock. 'Of course. . .that's what I'm here for.'

Fiona felt a familiar pang as for the umpteenth time she found herself regretting the times she was unable to be with her son. With Lilli close behind her she climbed down from the attic, and once back in the kitchen she brewed a badly needed cup of tea. As she was pouring the tea the telephone rang and Lilli disappeared into the hall to answer it, leaving Fiona sitting at the breakfast bar, her hands curled round her cup, staring out of the window at the small windswept garden beyond.

Seeing Paul Sheldon again had upset her more than she cared to admit. Years ago she had quite resigned herself to the fact that she would probably never again set eyes on him. Now it seemed that fate had cruelly decreed otherwise. She still hesitated over telling Lilli, wondering just how her mother would react.

Lilli had been very fond of Paul when she had first met him, when Fiona had brought him to the craft centre in Shrewsbury where her mother had a workshop. In fact, thought Fiona ruefully, they had seemed to strike up an immediate rapport with each other, but that was usually the way with Lilli. . .and with Paul for that matter, for they both possessed that most magical of qualities—charisma.

For a few wild, undisciplined moments she allowed her thoughts to wander back to the few times when she and Paul had been off duty at the same time and she had taken him home to Shrewsbury for the odd weekend. That had been when they had both been working at the same Birmingham teaching hospital, in the days before she qualified, when she had been living in the nurses' home and he was still a houseman. Those far-off, precious days before life had become complicated and painful.

Restlessly she stood up and wandered to the window, staring out with unseeing eyes at the few bare fruit trees and the thick wodges of dead black leaves that choked the flower borders, threatening to smother the few colourful patches of polyanthus.

She had coped. Somehow, with Lilli's help, she had coped; now she felt threatened again. She turned as she heard Lilli coming back into the kitchen, deciding that she would have to tell her, but she had no chance, for her mother was talking even before she was in the room.

'That was Charles on the phone; he's coming over for supper later,' she said, and there was no denying the breathless note of happiness in her voice. Charles Farnsworth was a don at the University, and just lately he and Lilli seemed to be seeing quite a lot of each other. Suddenly it didn't seem to Fiona to be the right moment to tell her mother about Paul Sheldon. Instead, she drained her cup, saying, 'I'll just go up and see what those boys are up to.'

'Very well, tell them tea won't be long,' replied Lilli.

As Fiona climbed the stairs, she heard her mother humming happily to herself.

All was quiet in Dominic's bedroom, and Fiona smiled as she saw the makeshift tent fashioned from her son's bedcovers and stretched between the wardrobe door and the edge of his desk.

'Is this a private game, or can anyone join in?' she asked. The covers shook furiously as a tousled ginger head appeared. 'Hello, Neil. . .is Dominic in there with you?'

The little boy laughed, his face red from the heat under the covers. 'Yes, we're commandos,' he said breathlessly, just as another small figure squirmed its way to the edge of the covers and stuck his head out.

'Hello, Mum,' he said.

Fiona felt the breath catch in her throat as she gazed down into a pair of eyes beneath a thatch of dark blond hair; eyes that were neither quite grey nor blue.

CHAPTER TWO

THE following morning Fiona left the house in Cathedral Close before either Dominic or her mother were awake. She walked briskly to the hospital, for it was another chilly March day with a cold biting wind. Nothing, however, could match the chill in her heart that morning as she anticipated the day ahead. For the first time since she'd joined the staff at St Catherine's Fiona was dreading going on duty.

She had spent a sleepless night trying to come to some sort of decision, but when morning finally came she was as confused as ever. As she turned into the main entrance of the hospital an ambulance passed her on its way to Casualty, its blue light flashing. In Reception one of the night porters called out a cheery greeting, then she stepped into the lift and pressed the button for the third floor and the Orthopaedic Unit.

Ten minutes later she was sitting in Sister's office with the rest of the staff while the night nurse gave her report. It appeared they'd had a fairly quiet night, apart from Mr Evans, who had still been in a great deal of pain.

'I informed Dr Aziz,' explained the staff nurse, 'and he gave Pethidine and increased his sedation.

After that he seemed more comfortable, but this morning he appears nauseous.'

She went on to report on all the other patients, finishing with Mrs Barnes, who, it appeared, had once again attempted to wander in the middle of the night. 'Dr Aziz has now prescribed Melleril in syrup form to try to calm her.'

The sister ended her report by mentioning two patients who were due for Theatre that morning, one with a fractured neck of femur and another for total hip replacement. Neither had been given anything by mouth since midnight.

As she finished speaking the telephone rang, and she answered it, then when she had replaced the receiver she pulled a face at Fiona. 'That was Kelly, one of your students for this morning. She's sick, says she won't be in.'

'Huh, more like a hangover,' grunted Marilyn. 'Wasn't there a do at the social club last night?'

Fiona stood up. 'Well, whatever it is, she won't be in, and as we were short-staffed anyway, I'll get on to the manager for a replacement.' Before she could lift the receiver, however, the phone rang again. This time it was Mrs Evans enquiring about her husband. Fiona did her best to reassure her, promising to give her husband her love and tell him that she would be in to see him later in the day, then, as the night staff prepared to leave, she set about allocating duties to her staff.

As the other nurses filed from the office to start bedmaking, Jill Markham hung back. With one hand on the door-handle, she stared keenly at Fiona. 'Are you all right?' she asked at last.

Fiona looked up sharply from the medication sheets she had been studying. 'Yes, of course,' she replied quickly. 'Why?'

Jill shrugged. 'Oh, nothing really, I just didn't think you looked yourself this morning.'

'I. . . I didn't sleep very well, that's all,' said Fiona. 'I expect I'll improve as the morning goes on.'

Jill grinned as she tried to pin up her unruly black hair under her cap. 'Yes, we'd better be on our best behaviour this morning!'

'Why?' Again Fiona answered more sharply than she had intended, and her friend glanced curiously at her.

'Well, we've got Dr Paul What's-is-name starting, haven't we?'

'Sheldon. . . Paul Sheldon. . .the new registrar, that's who you mean, isn't it?' Fiona asked impatiently.

'Yes, that's right.' Jill was having difficulty hiding her surprise now at Fiona's abruptness. 'What did you think of him?' she added in an obvious attempt to lighten the tension.

Again Fiona shrugged, trying to appear nonchalant but finding it extremely difficult, for any mention of his name set her pulses racing. 'He seemed OK, but you can never be sure at first, can you?'

'Oh, I don't know; if the students are anything to go by, they thought he was the best thing since sliced bread. Sue and Kelly reckoned he could understudy for Robert Redford, and I must admit I thought he was rather dishy.' Jill stared curiously at Fiona. 'Didn't you?' she added.

Fiona was saved from answering because the telephone rang again, and, as she lifted the receiver in relief, Jill, with a wave of her hand, disappeared to the linen-room. The call was from the duty officer in Casualty to check that they had a bed for a young man who had been brought in after his motorbike had been in collision with a lorry on his way to work.

'Will he be for Theatre this morning?' Fiona asked, and was informed that he would be included in Mr Rossington's list at eleven o'clock. Clearing the line, she dialled the nursing manager's office and put in her request for replacement staff, only to be told that the demand was very high that morning and there would be some delay.

With a sigh Fiona left the office and went to help the staff, first with bedmaking and washes, then, when the large meal trolley arrived, with breakfast.

Systematically she dealt with the familiar routine, and, even though they were short-staffed, the drug round at least was completed, when a porter who had come to change the oxygen cylinders casually announced that the bigwigs were on their way.

The consultant's round happened every morning, and until now Fiona had thought little of it; even since she had been acting ward sister she had taken it all in her stride, but today was different. Not only had she been on edge all morning, but as the hour approached she felt her nervousness increase at the thought of seeing Paul again. By the time she heard the group approaching down the corridor her heart was hammering alarmingly.

St Catherine's was a teaching hospital, and that morning there was quite a large group with Mr Rossington which included two housemen, several medical students and of course the new registrar.

Dr Sheldon looked cool and efficient and very, very handsome in his white coat. As they moved from bed to bed he hovered on the edge of the group, while Fiona, in spite of the fact that her mouth had gone very dry, gave an update of each case to Mr Rossington, who in turn explained certain procedures to the students.

They spent some time with Jim Evans, where Mr Rossington explained the operation he had performed on the man's spine, which had involved taking a bone graft from his hip and the fusing together of two vertebrae. He finally prescribed Omnopon, a strong analgesic, to help control the pain, Diazepam as a muscle relaxant and Temazepam as a night sedative, then stated that he wanted Mr Evans to have complete bed-rest for three weeks.

When the ward round was complete it was time for the consultant and the registrar to join the ward sister, or in this case the acting ward sister, in the office for coffee and further discussion.

Somehow Fiona contrived to conduct the whole

meeting without any direct personal contact with the new registrar as they discussed the new patient, David Amery, the victim of the motorcycle accident, who would shortly be going to theatre.

'You'll assist me on this one, Paul?' enquired Mr Rossington. 'It looks to be a challenging case.'

'Of course,' Paul replied, studying the notes that had come up from Casualty and which Fiona had handed him. 'I agree, it does look interesting; in fact it looks very similar to a case in which I was recently involved at my last hospital.'

'Really? Perhaps we could discuss it.' Mr Rossington stood up and prepared to leave the office, thanking Fiona, who gave a silent sigh of relief as Paul joined him. If all their future encounters could be that simple she would have little to worry about.

At the doorway, however, Paul paused and, looking back at her, he winked, then gave her the old heart-stopping smile she remembered so well. Then he was gone, leaving Fiona staring helplessly at the closed door.

Slowly she sank down into the chair, then as the door opened again almost immediately she sprang to her feet, thinking he had returned, but it was Marilyn Hughes who stood there.

'They've just brought the patient up from Casualty. . .' She trailed off as she caught sight of Fiona's expression, then she frowned. 'What's up?' she demanded suspiciously.

'Nothing. . .it's nothing,' Fiona replied quickly, picking up the case-notes from the desk.

'Did old Rossington give you a hard time?' There was a malicious gleam in Marilyn's eyes as she stared at Fiona.

'Of course not,' replied Fiona firmly. 'Now, can we get on?' There was no way she was going to give Marilyn the satisfaction of thinking there was anything wrong. She knew the other staff nurse only too well, and she would twist any situation to her advantage, especially where Fiona was concerned. It was common knowledge on the ward that Marilyn Hughes more then fancied her chances for the post of ward sister.

Somehow Fiona got through the rest of the morning: the list to go to the theatre, visits from physiotherapists and the dietician and the remainder of the ward routine.

At lunchtime she took herself off to the canteen on the fourth floor. She chose quiche and a salad, then carried her tray to a quiet corner by the window which was partly obscured from view by a large cheese plant. Carefully she set down her tray, transferring her lunch to the table, then with a sigh of relief she sat down.

She knew that the time had come when she had to pull herself together. She was usually so cool and was noted by her colleagues for her calm sense of efficiency. She couldn't now allow anything to jeopardise her chances of promotion, and that included the presence of the new registrar. The mere fact that Marilyn had noticed there was something wrong with her had been enough to goad Fiona into some sort of action. It just seemed so unfair that Paul Sheldon had chosen that particular time to walk back into her life.

Now that she'd had time to get over the initial shock, Fiona tried hard to be practical. Seven years was a long time, and during that time she had convinced herself that she had got over him. Equally, she reasoned, a good deal could have happened in seven years of his life. He might even be married. As the thought struck her, she found herself trying to remember whether he had said anything about being married when they had first spoken, but, apart from knowing that he'd asked if *she* was married, she found she could remember very little of what had been said at that first traumatic encounter.

She finished her meal and, thoughtfully stirring her coffee, she gazed out of the window which looked out over the attractive hospital gardens. Pale spring sunshine had broken through the clouds, considerably brightening the golds and purples of the crocuses that clustered beneath the large horse-chestnut trees, while in the flower borders delicate narcissi tossed and waved in the strong breeze.

For once, however, the beauty of the scene made no impression on Fiona as she battled with her thoughts and feelings. Finally she came to the conclusion that there need be very little reason for her to have any social contact with the new registrar other than on the ward. If he showed any signs of persistence she would just have to invent some other relationship, she thought, then, feeling decidedly better from her positive thinking, she sipped her coffee.

So lost had she become in her thoughts that she started as a shadow fell across her table and a voice said, 'May I join you?'

To her dismay, when she looked up it was to find Paul Sheldon smiling down at her, a slightly quizzical expression on his handsome features and his blond hair gleaming in a shaft of sunlight. Not waiting for an answer, he transferred his lunch to her table and, apparently taking her silence for assent, stood his tray against the wall, then sat down.

'So what's the food like?' he asked, eyeing his shepherd's pie and vegetables. 'It doesn't look too bad.'

'No, it's really quite good here,' Fiona heard herself say faintly.

He tucked in immediately, while she carried on drinking her coffee, trying to finish it as quickly as she could so that she could make her escape. He, however, seemed to have other ideas, for between mouthfuls he began to discuss the boy in the motorbike accident.

'He's lucky to be alive,' he commented, then added, 'He's in a bit of a mess, though. Got a long haul ahead of him. Lots of careful nursing from you and your girls, Fiona.' He looked up from his lunch and grinned, and, in spite of her earlier resolutions, she felt her heart doing crazy things again.

She swallowed. 'What were his injuries?' she

asked casually. Because he had started discussing work she didn't feel she could make such a rapid retreat as she had planned.

'Multiple fractures of both legs, fractured pelvis, ruptured spleen and a cracked collarbone. Still,' he raised his eyebrows in a hopeful expression, 'Rossington seems like a good man, so I'd say the lad has a fair chance.'

Fiona nodded. 'Yes, Mr Rossington is the best. In fact, we have an excellent team here; have you met the other two surgeons yet?'

'I've met Simpson but not Weatherall,' replied Paul, then, continuing enthusiastically, he said, 'I knew Simpson in London. We worked together for three years; in fact he recommended me for this post. So I would say I owe him one, wouldn't you?'

He smiled knowingly and Fiona felt a wave of panic, but, before she had the chance to say anything to steer him off the subject, he said, 'So when are you going to fill me in on what's been happening in your life?'

'What do you mean?' She threw him a startled glance and was even more disconcerted to find him watching her closely through half-closed eyes, his head slightly tilted to one side.

'Well, for a start, how do you come to be nursing here at St Catherine's?'

She shrugged slightly. 'It just felt time for a change, so we moved to Merstonbury. The job came afterwards.'

She realised her mistake as he set his knife and

fork down and stared at her enquiringly. 'We?' he asked softly.

She hesitated, then said, 'Yes, my mother and I.'

'Lilli?' He looked genuinely surprised, and she was reminded anew how well he and her mother had got along. 'Lilli's here in Merstonbury?'

She nodded, wishing he would stop asking questions. 'Yes, we live together,' she said at last, hoping that would be enough to satisfy his curiosity. But it seemed it had only increased his interest.

'Really?' He leaned forward, his lunch forgotten. 'And how is she?' His tone had softened.

'She's very well, thank you,' Fiona replied in the same non-committal fashion.

'Is she still painting?'

'Oh, yes, she's doing very well, as a matter of fact.'

He raised his eyebrows, waiting for her to continue, and she carried on, in spite of herself, for really she was very proud of Lilli. 'Yes, she's already had one exhibition in Merstonbury—at the local library. It was actually a shared one with another local artist, but it was so successful that she's now working towards another, this time on her own at the gallery in the High Street.'

'I'm very impressed, but it's no more than I would have expected. I always thought Lilli was very talented,' Paul said, pushing the remains of his meal away and turning his attention to his coffee.

Fiona was just thinking that it seemed like a

good opportunity to make her escape when he spoke again, softly but taking her by surprise. 'So that's filled me in as to what's been happening to Lilli, but it's told me nothing about you.'

She looked up and met his gaze, then, as evenly as she could, she said, 'There's little to tell.'

'In seven years?' He sounded faintly incredulous and she was forced to look away.

'You've quite obviously been pursuing your career,' he persisted. 'From what I've heard in the short time I've been here, there's no reason why you shouldn't be made up to sister.'

She shrugged slightly. 'It's what I'm hoping for, of course, but who can tell?'

'You must have worked very hard.' He inclined his head slightly in acknowledgement of her achievements.

'No more than you,' she retorted, then wished she'd kept her mouth shut as his eyes narrowed enquiringly.

'Although it doesn't surprise me,' she added, and there was a slight edge to her tone which he couldn't fail to notice. 'You always were very ambitious, Paul.'

He nodded slowly. 'That's true. . .' Then, quite suddenly, he said, 'Why didn't you keep in touch, Fiona?'

'I did——'

'What, a couple of letters and one Christmas card? Do you call that keeping in touch?' His tone was faintly reproachful and he continued before she had a chance to reply, 'I wrote several times, but you didn't reply, and you didn't return the calls I made to the nurses' home. . . Why, Fiona?'

She evaded his stare, looking beyond him and out of the window, wishing she could escape but knowing this questioning was inevitable and had to be faced sooner or later.

At last she allowed her eyes to meet his again. The gleam of amusement was missing this time, however, and in its place was a look that could almost be interpreted as one of injured enquiry.

She took a deep breath. 'Aren't you forgetting something, Paul?'

'I am? You tell me.' He looked puzzled now.

She hesitated, almost as if she found it impossible to put into words, then, when she finally spoke, she almost blurted out the words so that they sounded like an accusation. 'It was you who left, you who went away.'

He stared at her in silence, then gently he said, 'I'm quite aware of that, and I thought you understood my reasons.'

'Your reasons?' She allowed herself a short laugh. 'Oh, yes, I remember—your career. You told me you had to go to further your career, that you didn't want a serious relationship. That was right, wasn't it?' She arched her eyebrows, quite aware of the sarcasm she'd allowed to enter her tone.

He frowned. 'Well, yes, basically I suppose that was right, but I didn't think you would have wanted it to be so final. I thought under the circumstances we would have at least remained friends.'

'And what circumstances were those?' Somehow Fiona managed to meet his gaze, in spite of the fact that her knees were knocking together under the table.

He continued to stare at her, as if he was unable to believe the attitude she was taking, then at last he leaned towards her again and, lowering his voice so that none of the other occupants of the canteen could hear, said, 'As I said to you yesterday, Fiona, I always believed that what we had was very special.' When she didn't reply, he continued, 'Can you look at me, Fiona, and tell me I was wrong? Can you?'

She swallowed and forced herself to look at him again, hating herself for the sudden rush of emotion that felt as if it were melting her very bones. 'No, Paul,' she managed to say at last, 'I can't deny what was between us, and yes, it was very special, but it all happened a long time ago. Times change, people change.' She stood up, hoping that her knees wouldn't give way. 'You and I are different people now, Paul, and what we had between us was over a very long time ago.'

Briefly she was aware of the expression of pain that flitted across his features, then she turned and somehow managed to walk away from him and back to the ward.

CHAPTER THREE

'I ALWAYS thought you should have told him at the time,' said Lilli, as she settled herself more comfortably in the corner of the floral-patterned sofa and tucked her feet under her. Then, glancing curiously at her daughter, she said, 'Why didn't you, Fe?'

Fiona, who was sitting at a small writing-desk in the corner of their living-room, pretending to be busy, didn't look round. Instead she merely shrugged and said, 'I had my reasons.'

'I don't doubt that for one minute,' Lilli replied mildly. 'Just as I don't doubt that at the time your reasons seemed to you very valid. But I still think, no matter how valid those reasons, Paul Sheldon had the right to know he had a son.'

'Maybe, maybe not, but what you're saying, Lilli, is that he had the right to know then. Does he still have that right now, seven years later? Can you imagine what his reaction would be if he found out now?'

Lilli fell silent, a frown creasing her forehead as she deliberately linked and unlinked her small delicately shaped hands. 'Is there a chance that he may not stay at St Catherine's for very long? Perhaps he'll move on soon?' she asked hopefully at last.

Fiona shook her head. 'I wouldn't ho[ld] many hopes in that direction. As I told [you just] now, he's worked very hard for this position[, and I] can't see any reason why he should want to [let it] go.' She stood up and closed the writing-desk, then, almost unaware of her actions, she began to pace the living-room floor.

She had waited until after their evening meal and Lilli's report on Dominic's open day before telling her about Paul. Her mother's reaction, although fairly predictable, had been pleasurable interest at news of Paul Sheldon after so long, quickly followed by concern as she considered the implications.

'A man of Paul's intelligence will very quickly put two and two together when he knows about Dominic's existence,' said Lilli slowly.

Fiona stopped pacing and turned, staring at her mother. 'It doesn't need any intelligence,' she said abruptly. 'He'll only have to look in the mirror— the resemblance is there for anyone to see!'

'So what are you going to do?' asked Lilli anxiously.

Fiona sighed. 'I don't know. . . I just don't know.'

They remained silent for some moments, each busy with her own thoughts, then Lilli said, 'As far as I can see, you have three options.'

'Three?' Fiona stared at her incredulously. She'd been having difficulty finding one.

'Yes. One is that we uproot again and move on——'

'You're not serious? We've only just got settled here! Damn it, we're all happy—you at the gallery, Dominic at school and me—well, I've got the best job prospects I've ever had. I don't see why we should all be driven out because Paul Sheldon's decided to return!'

'All right, don't bite my head off. . . I thought you'd say that.' Lilli smiled. 'So that leaves two other options.' When Fiona remained silent, she went on, 'One is that you come clean and tell him all. . .' She paused as Fiona stirred uneasily. 'Oh, I know you may think that's impossible, but I don't believe you've thought it out sufficiently. Is it his anger you're afraid of?'

'No!' Fiona rounded sharply on her mother. 'No, it isn't that. . .'

'So what is it? Are you afraid he might start making claims on Dominic? Is that it?' Lilli probed gently when Fiona didn't reply.

At last Fiona sighed. 'Yes, I suppose that is it. I don't want him in Dominic's life. I've coped without him until now and I don't see why he should just walk back into our lives. After all, it was him who left, not me.'

'But you're talking as if he knew about Dominic,' said Lilli gently. 'He didn't, and, in all fairness to Paul, I firmly believe that if he had known, he wouldn't have left.'

'So what's the third option?' asked Fiona, choosing to ignore what her mother was saying.

'The third option? Well, that's simple. You carry on as if nothing had happened.'

'Hmm, that could be easier said than done, with Paul around. Already he's been asking far too many questions for my liking.'

'But there's no reason for him to come into contact with Dominic, is there? Surely it's going to be a matter of keeping your professional life and your social life completely separate?'

Fiona nodded doubtfully, then, pushing her hair back from her forehead in a weary gesture, she said, 'I need more time to think about it, but I'm tired now. I think I'll go to bed. Thanks for listening, though.' At the doorway she paused and looked back at her mother. 'Just as a matter of interest,' she said curiously, 'which of the three options would you take?'

'Me?' Lilli looked up quickly, but she didn't have to think about her answer. 'Oh, the second. . .most definitely, the second.'

Fiona trailed wearily up the stairs, feeling drained and exhausted. On the landing she paused at her son's bedroom door, then quietly she turned the handle.

Dominic was lying on his back, his arms spread-eagled, his hair damp and his long sooty eyelashes resting on his cheeks. For a long time Fiona stood and watched him, agonising over the decision that now faced her.

People had assumed that Dominic's father was dead, but once, about a year ago, Fiona had overheard her son talking to Neil and he'd told him that his daddy would be coming home one day. She hadn't corrected him at the time, thinking it might be better to wait until he was a little older before explaining that his father wouldn't be coming back. But now that very thing had happened; his father had come back, and she was torn over what decision she should make.

As she watched her son sleep she was reminded of how it had once been with Paul, and it was as if a knife turned in her heart as memories which she thought she had buried for ever rose to the surface.

Fiona had never believed in love at first sight. Not until she met Paul Sheldon, that was, for from the very moment her eyes had met his as he'd helped her into the punt that day on the river she had loved him.

She had loved walking with him, talking with him, simply being with him, and then as their relationship progressed with a speed that left her breathless she knew without a doubt that she was in love with him.

They had been heady days, full of fun and laughter, and so deeply in love was she that she didn't doubt for one moment that he felt the same way.

At the time she was living at the nurses' home, but she had been spending more and more time with Paul at his flat. He had seemed to want this as much as she had, and in fact if she had suggested returning to her room more often than not it had been he who had persuaded her to stay. That was why the shock when he had told her he was leaving would remain with her forever.

It had happened at the time when she had had

the first faint suspicions that she might be pregnant.

She had said nothing to Paul because not only did she want to be absolutely sure but she also was a little uncertain of his reaction. She had been reasonably certain that he would be as delighted as she, for their lovemaking had always been spontaneous and passionate.

On the other hand, she had known he would be surprised, for she had been taking a contraceptive pill. She had, however, been having a few problems with it, and her GP had recommended that she change to another brand. If she was pregnant it must have been during the change-over that she had conceived.

She could remember clearly every detail of the evening when Paul had told her he was going.

They had met as usual in the hospital social club for a drink after coming off duty, then, instead of going straight back to his flat as they usually did, he had suggested going for a walk.

Ironically it had been on the river-bank where they had first met that he told her he had been offered a position in a London hospital and he had accepted it because it was the next logical step to further his career. He had gone on to say that, while their relationship had meant a great deal to him, he felt that it had become more serious than he had intended. Fiona had listened to him in total disbelief, numbed by what she was hearing.

He had left a week later, by which time she had known for sure that she was pregnant. By that time she had also made the decision not to tell him. If he had decided he didn't want their relationship to continue there was no way she wanted him to feel obliged to return to her simply for the sake of the coming baby.

His decision to end their relationship had hurt her more than she could bring herself to admit. She had cleverly hidden her pain, even from Paul himself when he had said goodbye with promises that they would keep in touch and stay friends. She knew in her heart there was no way she could accept any half-measures with Paul; her love for him had been so intense that it could only be all or nothing.

When the time had come she had left the hospital and gone home to Lilli in Shrewsbury.

In spite of her reservations about Paul's being told, Lilli had stood by her through all the difficult times that followed. It had taken a long time to establish what they enjoyed today, and as Fiona stood in Dominic's bedroom and stared down at him she felt more than reluctant to jeopardise what they had.

And by the time she stole from the room and softly closed the door, she had made up her mind to take the third option. She had decided she would do everything in her power to prevent Paul Sheldon's finding out that he had a son.

Once Fiona had made her decision she found things easier to cope with than she had feared. On the occasions she came into contact with Paul at work she made it perfectly plain, by the coolness of her manner, that she wanted their relationship to be no more than a professional one. She also decided she would make it plain that she didn't want it to be common knowledge that they had known one another in the past.

But for the next few days she saw little of the new registrar. It seemed that most of his time was spent either in the operating theatre or in Out-patients. When he did arrive on the ward he was usually in the company of a consultant or a group of students, leaving little opportunity for personal conversation.

Patients came and went on Fiona's ward, then at the end of the week David Amery arrived back in the ward after his spell in Intensive Care follow-ing his operations. He still required very careful nursing, for not only was his body shattered, but his mind was also in a very depressed state.

Fiona spent as much time as she could with him, although in those early days after his accident he had very little to say.

On his first morning on the ward he received much attention during the consultant's round. He was lying flat with metal pins through both legs, which were in traction.

Mr Rossington asked David many questions, which seemed to tire him; he then discussed the case in detail with his students and with Paul Sheldon.

Fiona stood back, until Mr Rossington gestured to Paul to take over while he moved on to the next bed to talk to Mr Evans. Fiona found herself facing Paul across David's bed.

'Any problems, Staff Nurse?' he asked coolly, as he lifted the observation chart from the rail at the foot of the bed.

'Nothing serious,' she replied. 'We shall require a stronger analgesic for tonight, I would imagine. He's also suffering from constipation.'

'Very well, I'll write him up for some Lactulose, and he'll still be having Pethidine for the next two nights at least. Fluid output satisfactory? Good. Now, any other problems?' he asked as they moved away from David to join the others around Mr Evans's bed.

'He's very depressed,' she replied briefly.

'That's understandable. What's the family situation? Is there much support?'

'A rather hysterical mother, who doesn't seem to be helping very much. Oh, and his girlfriend, who's being allowed to visit later today.'

Paul pulled a face. 'Well, I suppose that could go either way—these affairs of the heart can be a morale-booster or a crashing disaster, don't you agree, Staff Nurse?'

For the briefest of moments she allowed her eyes to meet his, then she replied, 'Oh, quite definitely, Dr Sheldon.'

At that moment Mr Rossington turned to them with some comment about Mr Evans's treatment and, mercifully, the moment was lost. But that single incident, and the way in which Paul had phrased his question, brought it home to Fiona that she had been under some sort of illusion if she had imagined he had let the question of their past relationship drop.

The rest of that day proved to be very busy, with post-operative care for several patients, the discharge of two others and four admissions.

Fiona carefully supervised David's nursing: the changing of his dressings, his bed-bath and the two-hourly attention to his pressure-points, but throughout the day she was aware of his growing agitation as visiting time approached. She made a mental note to intercept his girlfriend before she saw him and prepare her for David's state of mind.

On that particular day Fiona was able to take her lunch break with her friend Jill Markham. They chose the same secluded corner of the canteen where Paul had joined Fiona a few days previously. Today there was no sign of him, much to Fiona's relief. She didn't want any socialising between herself, Jill and Paul, for there was a very real danger that Jill would mention Dominic.

This assumption proved correct, for they had barely taken a mouthful of their lasagne when Jill asked after Dominic.

'Oh, he's fine, thanks,' Fiona replied with a smile. 'He's growing up so fast that I can hardly keep up with him.'

'What is he now? Six, isn't it?'

Fiona nodded. 'Yes. He's just started judo lessons at the leisure centre on Saturday mornings.'

'Really?' Jill looked surprised. 'Isn't he a bit young for that?'

Fiona shook her head. 'No, they start very early. I remember someone once said to me that all children should be taught judo, and the earlier the better.'

'And how's he getting on at school?'

'Very well. He's in his second class at primary school. From what his teacher says it looks as if he's going to be quite bright.' Fiona said it modestly, playing down the fact that what his teacher had actually said was that Dominic was very bright indeed for his age.

'Must take after his mum,' Jill replied with a grin.

'Oh, I don't know about that,' said Fiona, pulling a face. 'I'm not particularly bright. I've always had to struggle to get where I wanted.'

'Don't we all?' said Jill with a sigh, then she added, 'I'm sure you'll get this sister's post, though, Fiona.'

Fiona shrugged. 'I just don't know. Marilyn Hughes stands a good chance.'

'The trouble with that one is her bedside manner, or rather her lack of it,' Jill replied drily, then, looking over Fiona's shoulder, she muttered, 'Talk of the devil. . .don't look now, but our mutual friend has just come in, and guess who she has in tow?'

Fiona shook her head.

'None other than our very own registrar, Dr Paul Sheldon—well, she certainly didn't waste any time there, did she? In fact, I heard rumours in the club last night that she was after him.'

Fiona felt a pang at her friend's words, and she was forced to remain silent.

Jill, however, didn't seem to notice anything and, keeping her voice lowered, she went on, 'I also heard that he happens to be a bachelor. . .can you believe it, with those looks? Anyway, it seems Marilyn fancies her chances with him—either that, or she thinks if she gets on the right side of him he'll put in a word for her over the sister's post.' She gave Fiona a wicked smile. 'Perhaps you'd better get in there, Fiona.'

'I don't think that's my style,' said Fiona with a faint smile, then became aware that her friend had set down her fork and was staring curiously at her.

'No, it isn't your style, is it?' Jill said at last. 'But having said that, I'm not really sure what is.'

'What do you mean?' Fiona looked startled, but at the same time was suddenly conscious out of the corner of her eye that Paul and Marilyn had carried their lunch to another table in the window and that Paul had seen her and was trying to catch her attention.

'Well, you have very little social life, do you?' When Fiona didn't reply, Jill continued, 'For instance, whenever there's anything on at the social club I can very rarely persuade you to come.'

Fiona smiled. 'I have Dominic to consider.'

'I know that, but you also have your own life to live,' Jill said gently. Then, more brightly, she added, 'Still, you will be coming to old Jenky's retirement dinner, won't you?'

Fiona nodded. 'Yes, I've already asked my mother to look after Dominic for that.'

'Talking of Dominic,' Jill went on, apparently oblivious to the nervous glance that Fiona threw in Paul Sheldon's direction, 'I have my nephews coming to visit soon, and they're about Dominic's age; suppose we have a day out somewhere— perhaps the zoo or the Adventure Park?'

'That would be great, Jill.' Fiona brightened up. 'Dominic would love it. I do worry that he doesn't have enough company of his own age.'

'Right, that's settled, then.' Jill glanced at her watch and pushed her cup and saucer away. 'Oh, well, it's back to the grindstone now.'

She stood up, and Fiona followed her from the canteen, only too aware as they passed the table occupied by Paul and Marilyn that he followed her with his eyes. She, however, didn't glance in his direction, giving him no reason to suppose that she had even been aware he had been there.

Towards the end of her shift there was a crisis on the ward when one of their elderly patients who had been to Theatre earlier in the day suffered a cardiac arrest. While Marilyn began cardiac massage, Fiona telephoned the crash team, and it was while they were attending to the patient in the female side of the ward that David Amery's girlfriend arrived unnoticed.

The cardiac patient failed to respond to all attempts to revive her, and it was while Fiona was caught up in the procedures that always followed a death on the ward that she happened to see a young girl practically run from the men's ward.

It was quite obvious that she was crying and in a very distressed state, and when Fiona attempted to approach her she pushed past her and ran down the corridor.

'Damn!' muttered Fiona as she stared after her. 'That's just what I wanted to avoid.' With a sigh she beckoned to one of the students and instructed her to take over what she had been doing, then, taking a deep breath, she walked out of her office and into the men's ward.

CHAPTER FOUR

DAVID was lying with his face turned towards the wall, and even when Fiona drew the curtains around his bed he didn't turn to look at her.

'I just want to check the areas around the pins in your legs, David,' she said in as matter-of-fact a tone as she could. She lifted back his bedcovers, and all the while it took to remove his dressings, cleanse and apply fresh medication he didn't once turn his head. She talked steadily to him throughout the whole procedure in spite of his lack of response, but it wasn't until she had nearly finished that she caught the glint of tears on his cheek.

Her heart went out to him, for if his girlfriend had rowed with him—or even finished their relationship—in view of his injuries, she knew how he must be feeling. She tried, however, to keep up her slightly brisk, almost impartial air, feeling that this was the right approach.

As she tidied the dressing trolley she asked quietly, 'Do you want to talk about it, David?'

Still he didn't answer, so gently she persisted, 'It does help, you know, sometimes, to talk things out.'

His face remained turned to the wall, and Fiona was just thinking she'd failed miserably when very slowly he turned his head. He was a handsome boy with rich auburn hair and hazel eyes which, when he laughed, would light up with merriment, but at this moment Fiona was struck by the bleak, hopeless expression in their depths.

He stared at her without speaking for a long moment, then deliberately he said, 'Would you mind just going away and leaving me alone?'

Fiona winced at the bitterness in his tone. 'David, I do know how you're feeling. . .believe me,' she said in a last attempt to gain his confidence.

Again his pain-filled eyes met hers and for a moment she thought he was going to talk, then slowly he said, 'You don't know what you're talking about. You haven't got any idea how I'm feeling.'

'Well, I know all about rejection,' she said drily, as she paused with one hand on the rail of the trolley, looking down at him.

'Rejection? What's rejection got to do with it?' For a moment he looked almost angry, but at least he was talking, so Fiona carried on quickly.

'I saw your girlfriend rushing out just now and she looked pretty upset. I'm afraid I just put two and two together.'

'Yes, and came up with five,' he said sharply.

'I don't understand.' She looked at him curiously, noting the white lines of pain on his face. 'I thought perhaps she'd finished your relationship.'

'Well, that was just where you were wrong,

because it was me who finished it, not Tracy.'
Again he turned his face to the wall.

Fiona stared at him, then gently she touched his
shoulder, making him flinch at the unexpected
gesture. 'But why, David?' she asked gently. 'Why
did you do that?'

She saw the muscles of his throat constrict as he
struggled to control his emotions, and she
remained silent, giving him time.

'She doesn't want to be saddled with me now,'
he muttered.

'Don't you think you should let her be the judge
of that?'

'She doesn't understand. . .she doesn't know
what it'll be like. . .it's for the best this way.'

'Well, from what I saw it didn't look as if it was
the best for her. She seemed extremely upset,' said
Fiona firmly. Again David turned to look at her
and this time there was a glimmer of something
new in his eyes, then it was gone and the bleak-
ness returned. 'She may feel like that now,' he
said harshly, 'but later, she'll be relieved.'

Quietly Fiona drew up a stool and sat down
beside him. 'And how have you reached that
conclusion?' she asked.

'Well, I'm going to be a right drag, aren't I? It's
quite likely I won't even walk again, let alone
anything else. What sort of prospect is that? What
future do I have to offer any girl, for God's sake?'

'You don't know that at the moment—why, Dr
Sheldon was only saying this morning that he
hopes you'll make a full recovery.'

'Yes, but on the other hand there's a chance I'll end up in a wheelchair.' He glared angrily at Fiona and when she didn't answer he demanded, 'Well, isn't there?'

'Yes, David, there is that chance,' she looked at him steadily as she spoke, 'but I don't believe that taking this defeatist attitude is going to help anyone, least of all you or Tracy.'

'I've told her not to come again,' he muttered. 'She only gets upset seeing me like this.'

'Well, I think you're making a big mistake. Tracy wants to be with you, I'm sure, and you shouldn't prevent her from coming.' With a flourish Fiona swept back the curtains—only to find Paul Sheldon standing at the foot of the adjacent bed. From his expression she could see that he had overheard her conversation with David.

'I'm sorry, Dr Sheldon,' she said, pushing the trolley out of his way, 'I didn't realise you were waiting to see David.'

'That's quite all right, Staff.' Paul smiled his casual easy smile that seemed to charm everyone. 'I'm sure you've been doing the patient more good than I can.'

To her dismay she felt the colour tinge her cheeks, and lowering her head, she pushed the trolley from the ward, only too aware of Paul's eyes on her as she left.

Fiona saw little of Paul for the rest of the week, much to her relief, while on her ward David's progress was very slow, hampered, Fiona was certain, by the visits from his over-protective mother and the absence of Tracy. But it did seem she had made a little headway with him in her attempt to talk, because from that day on, he seemed to respond to Fiona and communicate with her more than with anyone else.

The following weekend Fiona was off duty, and on Saturday morning it was her turn to go to the precinct to do the weekend shopping.

Neil's mother, Jane, had taken both boys to the local leisure centre for their judo lesson and Lilli had gone to the wholesaler's with Charles Farnsworth to buy art materials.

There was a heavy drizzle falling as Fiona finished her shopping, and she was just leaving the precinct laden with two heavy bags when a car pulled to a halt beside her. She glanced at the car, but, not recognising it, she walked on. Seconds later a sudden shout made her stop and look back.

The driver had got out of the car and was leaning on the open door. With a jolt she realised it was Paul Sheldon.

'Don't you acknowledge your old friends in the street any more?' He grinned, and Fiona, feeling uncomfortable, changed her shopping-bags over.

'I'm sorry, I didn't realise it was you,' she said, glancing at the car, a silver-grey Rover, and mentally comparing it with the clapped-out old Morris he'd used to drive.

Paul, seeming to interpret her glance, said, 'Those bags look pretty heavy—come on, let me give you a lift.' Without giving her a moment to protest, he had stepped forward, taken the bags from her hands and stowed them in the boot, then was opening the passenger door for her and standing back so she could get into the car.

It was while he was taking his seat and fastening his safety-belt that she felt panic set in. Wildly she glanced at him, wondering if she could change her mind and tell him that she still had more shopping to do. But if she did he would probably say he would wait for her. Almost as if he sensed her panic he looked at her, a quizzical expression on his face.

Vaguely it registered that he was wearing a tracksuit and that his hair was wet, more so than if he had merely been caught in the rain, and it briefly crossed her mind that he had probably been swimming at the local baths. As her eyes met his she felt her mouth go dry, and she swallowed and looked away.

'Well?' he asked suddenly, and she threw him a startled glance.

'I'm sorry?' She frowned.

'If I'm to take you home, I need to know where I'm going.'

'Oh—oh, yes. It's Cathedral Close. . .do you know it?'

Paul shook his head. 'No, but I imagine if I head in the general direction of the Cathedral I'll find it?'

Fiona nodded, then bit her lip, cursing the fact that he had come along just at that moment. This was exactly what she had wanted to avoid. She didn't want him to know where she lived, and throughout the short drive she agonised that Jane might have got back with the boys and be outside the house waiting for her. She was just wondering if she could persuade him to drop her off at the corner when they reached the Close and he pulled into the square, looking up with interest at the neat row of stone cottages.

Mercifully there was no sign of Jane's car. 'Is it one of these?' he asked. 'They look nice. . .which one is yours?'

Numbly she pointed, indicating her home, and he drew to a halt, switching off the engine.

Surely he didn't expect her to ask him in? Wildly she looked around, then attempted to unfasten her seat-belt, but her fingers shook and she found herself fumbling with the clasp.

'Here, let me do that.'

Fiona stiffened as Paul leaned across and she suddenly found his hand covering hers. She looked up and found his face only inches from her own and, for one wild, incredible moment of *déjà vu*, it was as if the last seven years hadn't happened.

He was so close that if she had leaned forward only slightly her lips could have touched his and once again they could have shared a kiss, just as it had been before. Her eyes flickered from his lips, firm and beautifully shaped above a slightly cleft chin, to his eyes, neither quite blue nor grey, then back again to his mouth.

Almost imperceptibly he moved forward and

just when it seemed inevitable, when his lips almost touched hers, she pulled away.

Paul sharply drew in his breath, releasing her seat-belt while she struggled with the door catch. As the door swung open and she attempted to get out, he said quietly, 'Do I take it I'm not being invited in for coffee?'

Fiona hesitated on the pavement, knowing how rude she must appear to him when he had taken the trouble to bring her home, but at the same time knowing that at any second Jane would be rounding the corner with Dominic in her car. Before she had the chance to frame an excuse, however, Paul got out of the car and went round to the boot.

She had almost forgotten her shopping, so great was her haste to get safely inside the house. As Paul lifted the bags out, he glanced up at the house.

'I was hoping to see Lilli again,' he began.

'Oh, she isn't in,' said Fiona hurriedly, then added, 'She'll be home soon, but she's bringing a client with her, something about a portrait, I believe, so I'm afraid I can't ask you in just now, Paul.'

It was a lame excuse and she knew it, but it would have to suffice, as time was running out. For one awful moment she thought he was going to continue talking, then he simply shrugged, slammed the boot shut and climbed back into the car. Winding down his window, he said softly, 'Some other time, then, Fiona?'

Wordlessly she nodded and bent down to pick up her shopping, then paused as he added, 'Besides, I want to talk to you some time.'

'Oh, oh, yes, all right,' she said, willing at that moment to agree to anything if only he would drive away.

With a sigh of relief she watched as he started the engine and the car drew smoothly away. He drove round the Close and out on to the main road on the far side. As his car disappeared Jane's car turned into the square with the two boys in the back seat.

'Hello, Fiona.' Jane got out of the car and opened the rear door for the boys. 'Sorry we're a bit late, I had to go to the post office on the way back.'

'Oh, that's all right,' replied Fiona, wishing her knees would stop shaking. 'I've only just got back myself.'

'Hi, Mum!' Dominic hurtled past her up the path with Neil at his heels, then on the doorstep they had to wait for her to unlock the door.

'Did you have a good lesson?' she asked as she put one of the bags down and searched in her pocket for her keys.

'Super—we've got a new teacher, haven't we, Neil?'

'Yes, better than old Stinky Saunders,' said Neil, and both boys went off into fits of giggles.

'We'll have less of that sort of talk, thank you,' said Jane. 'Mr Saunders is a very nice man—he'd have to be, to give up his Saturday mornings to teach you lot.'

'He's still stinky, though,' said Dominic, and, in the middle of another fit of giggles, Jane bent down to pick up Fiona's bag and the two boys streaked past Fiona into the house.

'Good grief, Fiona, whatever have you got in here? How did you manage to carry this lot back from the precinct?'

'Actually, I had a lift. Oh, thanks, Jane, just put it over there and I'll get the kettle on. I expect you could do with a coffee? Have you seen my scarf?' Fiona glanced round. 'I hope I haven't lost it; it's the silk one that Lilli gave me.'

'So who gave you a lift?' Jane perched on one of the stools in front of the pine breakfast bar in the kitchen while the two boys rushed up the stairs, intent on some adventure of their own.

Fiona paused with the kettle in one hand. 'Oh, no one really, just the registrar at the hospital.'

'No one, she says!' Jane rolled her eyes. 'Just any old registrar. I suppose you're going to tell me next that he's tall, dark and handsome and single into the bargain?'

'Well, he's not dark, for a start,' Fiona sniffed, and, taking down two mugs, put a spoonful of instant coffee in each.

'So what are you saying, that he's tall, fair and single?'

'Yes, that's about it.'

Jane stared at her, an incredulous expression on her face. 'Next, you're going to say he's handsome as well, right?'

Fiona nodded weakly. 'Well, now that you ask,

yes, I suppose he is, but. . .oh, there's the door-bell. It's probably Lilli, she must have forgotten her key. Pour that orange juice for the boys, will you, Jane? I won't be a minute.'

She hurried through to the hall and pulled open the front door.

Paul Sheldon stood on the step. In his hand he carried her silk scarf.

For a moment they simply stared at each other, then he said, 'You dropped this in the car. I thought you might be worrying that you'd lost it.'

Irrelevantly she noticed that his hair had now dried and, as it had always used to, had dried slightly wavy. She remembered that from the days when they had shared a shower together, some-times before, sometimes after making love.

Almost as if he read her thoughts, the familiar gleam of amusement came into his eyes, and Fiona shook herself back to the present. Then she stiff-ened as Jane suddenly spoke from the kitchen doorway and Paul looked over her shoulder, no doubt imagining he would see Lilli.

'Shall I give them a shout, Fiona, or shall I. . .?' She trailed off as she caught sight of Paul.

'Oh, I'm sorry, I thought you were Lilli.' She glanced at Fiona, obviously expecting an introduction.

'This is Paul Sheldon,' she said abruptly. 'Paul, this is Jane Cotton. It was Paul who gave me a lift home. I left my scarf in his car and he's very kindly returned it.' Seeing the speculative look in Jane's eyes, she turned back to Paul and determinedly, with one hand on the doorlatch, she said, 'Well, thank you very much, Paul. I'll see you on Monday.' Before he had the chance to say anything further, she firmly closed the door.

For a split second, weak with relief, she leaned against it, then glanced anxiously up the stairs, but for once the boys were quiet. She began to walk towards the kitchen, then stopped when she saw the look of astonishment on Jane's face.

'Whatever did you do that for?'

'What?' Fiona queried casually, knowing full well what her friend meant.

'Send him away! After all, it isn't every day I get the chance to have coffee with a handsome doctor—it's all right for you, you probably do it every day, but that sort of chance doesn't come my way too often, and oh, boy, was he gorgeous! Why——'

'Surgeon,' interrupted Fiona, as she picked up her mug of coffee and settled herself on a stool.'

'What?'

'He's a surgeon as well as a doctor.'

'Oh, he's a surgeon, she says!' Jane rolled her eyes, and Fiona was finally forced to laugh.

'I'm sorry, Jane, really I am. I know you don't get to meet that many eligible men since your divorce, but I had my reasons for not inviting that particular man into my home—believe me,' Fiona stressed as Jane still looked sceptical, 'he's bad news.'

Jane shrugged and curled her hands round her

mug. 'Oh, well, never mind, I'll just have to take your word for it.'

Both girls glanced up as the front door opened again and Lilli appeared with a tall, silver-haired man behind her. They were both loaded with canvases and plastic carrier-bags.

'Oh, here you are—let me help.' Fiona hurried forward to take some of the packages, while Jane put the kettle on again and the boys hurtled down the stairs to the accompaniment of a series of whoops and squeals.

'Did you get everything you wanted?' asked Fiona, as Charles set down a stack of the heavier canvases against the kitchen wall.

He nodded. 'I think so. We would have been here a bit sooner, but we've been outside talking to Paul Sheldon.'

In the silence that followed Fiona froze, then, turning slowly, she caught Lilli's eye. Her mother very slightly shook her head. It was barely perceptible, but it was enough to let Fiona know that Charles was unaware of the situation. Taking a deep breath, Fiona said, 'I didn't know you knew Paul Sheldon, Charles.'

'Oh, yes, his father and I were at Cambridge together. We aren't exactly close friends, but we've kept in touch over the years. Paul was saying he's taken a new post at the hospital on your unit, Fiona—isn't that a coincidence? He turned to Lilli. 'I must say, my dear, Paul seemed very pleased to see you.'

Jane frowned, as if the conversation was getting

beyond her, and Fiona held her breath, but Lilli made some non-committal reply and the moment was further saved by Dominic asking if they could switch on the television in the sitting-room to watch *Batman*.

It wasn't until much later, after Jane and Neil and Charles Farnsworth had gone and Dominic had gone up into the attic with Lilli to help her sort out her supplies, that Fiona had the time to consider the implications of the morning's events.

Until that day she had begun to hope that her fears that Paul would find out about Dominic were unfounded. She had almost come to the conclusion that it would be easy to keep her private life separate from her professional one, and that there was no reason why the two paths should ever cross. But it seemed that she hadn't bargained for the little everyday occurences that happened for no apparent reason, like being offered a lift in the rain or leaving her headscarf in someone's car. But even those incidents, disastrous as they had almost been, hadn't convinced Fiona that she might not still get away with her plan.

What she hadn't bargained for was the power of coincidence; the chance meeting and the cruel twist of fate that had made a close friend of her mother's such a danger. For whoever could have foreseen that Paul would have actually known Charles Farnsworth? And now that he knew there was a connection, what was to stop him trying to pursue the acquaintance, including herself and Lilli in the process?

As Fiona rinsed the coffee-mugs, then sorted out Dominic's judo clothes for washing, the troubled thoughts chased themselves round in her mind and she realised that the course she had chosen to take was by no means going to be an easy one.

As if in an echo to her own thoughts, Lilli's voice suddenly intruded.

'It's all going to be more difficult than you thought, isn't it, darling?'

Fiona turned sharply and stared at Lilli standing in the doorway, then suddenly her defences crumbled and, clutching her son's white judo tunic to her, she wailed, 'Oh, Lilli, whatever am I going to do?'

CHAPTER FIVE

FIONA awoke on the following Monday morning to a thick blanket of fog that even obscured the Cathedral. She shivered, pulled her bathrobe tightly around her, then hurried to shower and dress. She knew from bitter experience what a foggy Monday morning could mean on an orthopaedic unit.

She was later proved right, for, after arriving on the unit and taking the report, she found that Casualty had one case after another for Orthopaedics. Two women were victims of a particularly nasty pile-up on the M4 in which another woman, a man and a small child had been killed, and the other cases, although not so serious, required just as much nursing skill.

It was the start of what was to be a very busy morning, and, although Fiona had been dreading seeing Paul after the episode on Saturday, she found that as soon as she set foot on the ward she had no time to think of anything other than the job in hand.

It was Marilyn Hughes's turn to be acting sister in charge with Fiona as her senior staff nurse, and with one student off with a stomach bug, another on leave and a third with boyfriend troubles, both women were stretched to their professional limits.

By mid-morning, even before the consultant's round, the ward was full. Amongst the long-stay patients Jim Evans was progressing well but still on bed-rest; there were problems with Mrs Barnes, whose hip was proving slow to heal, and David Amery continued to be withdrawn and uncooperative.

While Fiona was helping an auxiliary nurse with David's bed-bath and dressings, Marilyn came in with a phone message from his mother, and at the same time Stuart McVey, the chief physiotherapist, arrived.

'So how's it going, then?' asked the big red-bearded Scot, receiving barely more than a nod from his patient in reply.

Stuart caught Fiona's eye and gave a slight grimace, but Marilyn, who was in an officious mood and anxious to exert her authority, said, 'David is doing very well. He just needs to help himself a little more.'

At her words David, who had just begun to talk to Fiona about a programme that he'd heard on his radio, turned his face to the wall, and Fiona glared at Marilyn in exasperation.

'Well, lad, perhaps we'll have a little chat when these ladies have finished with you, how's that?'

'Dr Sheldon is very pleased with David,' remarked Fiona as she straightened her patient's bedclothes and adjusted his traction weights.

'Ah, Dr Sheldon,' said Stuart. 'He's a good man, is that one. But you'd know all about that, Staff, wouldn't you?' His blue eyes twinkled as he stared at Fiona across the bed.

Marilyn, who had turned away, stopped at his words and looked over her shoulder.

'Whatever do you mean?' Fiona tried to sound casual, but her heart was suddenly hammering.

'Well, a little bird told me that you and our Dr Sheldon were pretty friendly at one time.'

Only too conscious of Marilyn's hostile stare, Fiona gave a nonchalant shrug. 'Oh, I wouldn't say that. We simply worked at the same hospital in Birmingham, that's all.'

She was saved from further interrogation by the arrival on the ward of the consultant and his entourage, which included Paul Sheldon, but, as it was Marilyn who was acting sister that morning and not her, Fiona was able to make her escape.

Marilyn Hughes, however, was not one to let the information about Paul Sheldon and Fiona rest, and later when Fiona was writing up a report in the office she tackled her about it.

'You never said you knew Dr Sheldon before,' she said accusingly.

'You never asked,' replied Fiona.

'I would have thought it was the kind of thing you would have mentioned when he first arrived.' Marilyn took some papers from the desk as she spoke, then looked suspiciously at Fiona as she added, 'That is, of course, unless you had anything to hide.'

Fiona sighed. 'No, Marilyn, there wasn't anything to hide. We simply worked in the same hospital, that's all.'

'It's odd that he didn't mention it either.' It was quite obvious that Marilyn wasn't going to let the matter drop.

'I don't see anything odd about it—besides, he must have mentioned it to someone.'

'What do you mean?'

'Well, Stuart McVey knew, didn't he? And I certainly haven't told anyone.'

Marilyn still looked far from convinced when she left the office, leaving Fiona to reflect on the fact that once again her previous relationship with Paul Sheldon was causing waves in her life. This time she had no doubt that it was because Marilyn herself was interested in him, if recent rumours were anything to go by. She had no idea how she would cope if a relationship developed between Paul and Marilyn. She decided she would just have to cross that bridge when she came to it. It was just another potentially explosive situation, similar to the one that had been created at the weekend.

Once again Lilli had urged her to reconsider telling Paul everything, and when she had refused Lilli had voiced her fears about Charles Farnsworth.

'Should I tell him?' she had asked Fiona as they had walked on the Common on Sunday afternoon, with Dominic running ahead flying his dragon kite.

Fiona had thrust her hands into the pockets of her waxed jacket and shook her head. 'No, I don't think there's any need.'

'But he seems to know Paul rather well—suppose he happens to mention the fact that you have a son?'

Fiona had shrugged. 'That's a chance I'll have to take. He may never say anything.'

Lilli had dropped the matter then, but had still looked doubtful.

Now, as Fiona finished her report, she began to feel as if a net were closing around her. She was just replacing the cap on her pen when Jill put her head round the door.

'All set for tomorrow night?' she asked.

Fiona frowned.

'Wakey, wakey—the dinner for Olive Jenkins at the Grand Hotel! Honestly, Fiona, I don't know what's got into you lately, you seem so vague.'

Fiona forced a smile. 'I'm OK, just a bit tired, that's all, and of course I hadn't forgotten Olive's do. I'm quite looking forward to it, in fact; it's not every night we get to go to a dinner-dance at the Grand, is it?'

'We have old Henry Rossington to thank for that, or so I've heard. Apparently he thinks very highly of Olive.'

'Well, I'm glad. She's one of the best, is our Sister Jenkins, and I for one will be sorry to see her go,' replied Fiona as she prepared to go for her lunch.

'Even if you get her job?' Jill gave a wicked chuckle and Fiona pulled a face at her. As they left the ward Fiona reflected that at least she wouldn't have to worry about Paul's being at the dinner. He

hardly knew Sister Jenkins, and it seemed highly
unlikely that he would be asked to join in her
retirement party.

But Fiona had reckoned without the generous
spirit of Henry Rossington, who would never have
dreamt of excluding a member of his team from an
important event, especially a new member who
had yet to meet many of his colleagues socially.

Almost the first person she saw on stepping into
the foyer of the Grand Hotel was Paul Sheldon,
and the message she read in his eyes was one of
undisguised admiration.

She had, it was true, taken great pains with her
appearance, in spite of the fact that she was
wearing her one and only little black dress which
she kept for these occasions. Her hair she had
fluffed out into a curly bob, and she had borrowed
Lilli's pearl choker necklace and drop earrings. She
knew she was looking her best, a fact confirmed
by Paul's expression, and even though she was at
first dismayed to find him there she was also
relieved she had made an effort.

As they moved from the hotel foyer into the
cocktail bar for pre-dinner drinks Fiona had a
chance to study Paul unobserved while he was in
conversation with a group of his colleagues. She
had forgotten just how handsome he looked in
evening dress, his fair hair a perfect foil for his dark
suit. He looked easy and relaxed as he laughed
and joked, becoming the object of more than one

female glance as the members of the party assembled.

Yet again Fiona found herself marvelling at how little he had changed—and what changes had occurred only seemed to have made him more attractive, she thought ruefully.

'Hey, where were you?'

At the sound of Jill's voice Fiona looked up sharply, almost spilling her drink. 'I'm sorry?'

'You were miles away! I was chatting away and I swear you haven't heard a word I've been saying. Honestly, I don't know what's got into you lately! You just haven't been yourself. If I didn't know you better I'd say you were in love.' She looked quite injured, and Fiona was forced to laugh.

'I'm sorry, Jill, really I am. Now what was it you were saying?'

'I've forgotten now after all that. Oh, I know what it was—I was saying look at old Buchanan's outfit. It looks as if she's been to Oxfam. With all her money you'd think she could have found something better than that, wouldn't you?'

Fiona glanced across the bar to where a little group of sisters were chatting to Olive Jenkins, the guest of honour. She found she had to stifle a smile as she saw what her friend had been referring to. Audrey Buchanan, Olive Jenkins's arch-enemy, who would now be the senior sister on the unit, was clad in a hideous creation in brown and yellow brocade.

Quickly Fiona looked away, and as she did so

she caught Paul's eye and by the glint of amusement she saw there she knew he too was busy summing up the situation.

Their meal of smoked salmon mousse followed by roast pheasant and a mouthwatering champagne syllabub dessert was served against a background of soft music in the sumptuous Gainsborough Room with its gold and cream décor and deep pink velvet curtains.

Fiona had made up her mind to enjoy herself in spite of Paul's presence, for it wasn't often that she was entertained in such style, but through the meal she worried that someone might enquire after her son, and at the same time she was conscious of Paul's eyes upon her. He was seated further down the table from her, but he was on the opposite side, so it wasn't difficult for him to watch her.

Marilyn Hughes had somehow contrived to be seated on his left, and she too seemed to be aware of how often his gaze strayed down the table towards Fiona, for she constantly tried to claim his attention. She was looking flamboyant and slightly exotic in a scarlet, off-the-shoulder dress, her dark hair teased and waxed into a tousled modern style. On the few occasions that Fiona allowed herself a glance in that particular direction Marilyn seemed to be gazing adoringly at Paul and fluttering what could only be a set of false eyelashes.

Sister Olive Jenkins basked in the tributes from her colleagues which followed the dinner and was quite overcome with the presentations, a camera from the management, an oil-painting from Henry Rossington and his staff and a set of garden furniture from her own staff. She was misty-eyed when she made her thank-you speech, and was seen to blush for what her nurses were convinced was the first time ever when Mr Rossington gave her a kiss on the cheek and said he hated to see her go.

'She's always had a soft spot for old Henry,' whispered Stuart McVey in Fiona's ear.

'So I believe.' Fiona smiled and sipped her liqueur, which had been served with coffee after the meal.

'Uh-uh, looks like the entertainment is about to begin.' Stuart nodded towards a raised dais at the end of the room where a group had taken their places. A small dance-floor fronted the dais, and as the group broke into the strains of the latest Chris de Burgh number Stuart took Fiona's hand and before she had the chance to catch her breath, let alone protest, he had led her on to the floor, to the encouragement of the rest of their party.

They circled the floor a couple of times, then after a ripple of applause from the others they were joined by several other couples, Paul and Marilyn among them. Stuart was an excellent dancer, and after a while Fiona felt herself relax and begin to enjoy herself. As the evening went on she found she was never short of a partner, with even the great Henry Rossington asking her for a waltz.

It was getting quite late and the music smoochy

when Fiona, dancing again with Stuart, caught Paul's eye over Stuart's shoulder. He was dancing with Marilyn, and with a pang Fiona noticed that he was holding her very close. She quickly looked away, but there had been something in his expression that made her look back again. This time their glances locked and held, with both of them rendered incapable of looking away. Luckily their partners seemed oblivious to what was happening, for as the number ended Paul led Marilyn back to her seat, but almost before she had the chance to sit down he had returned to the dancefloor and claimed Fiona as she and Stuart left the floor.

Wordlessly, still mesmerised by that significant stare, she stepped into the circle of his arms.

The dress she was wearing had a very low-cut back, and the touch of his hand on her bare flesh was electric. Helplessly they stared at each other, and once again, like the moment in his car, Fiona experienced an overwhelming sense of *déjà vu* as the years seemed to melt away and the past caught up with them.

With a sigh Paul pulled her closer, and in spite of all her firm resolutions she leaned against him and briefly closed her eyes. Everything about him seemed the same, his touch, his smell, his voice and the very feel of him, and as they moved slowly, sensuously to the music, Fiona allowed herself the luxury of reliving the past.

For her there had never been anyone to remotely take his place. She had of course been on dates, but she had never allowed a serious relationship to develop. This, she knew, was partly because of Dominic, but now she was finally forced to admit it was mainly because of the man in whose arms she found herself once more—the man she still loved.

For a few precious moments it was as if time ceased to exist, the lights were dimmed and Fiona was totally oblivious to everyone else as Paul lowered his head, his cheek against hers.

It wasn't until the tempo changed slightly that she gradually became aware of her surroundings again and she realised that one or two couples were beginning to take their leave as it approached midnight.

'Do you think,' murmured Paul softly against her ear, 'that anyone would notice if we were to slip quietly away?'

Fiona stirred and looked up into his eyes, recognising the expression she saw there, an expression she had seen only too often in the past, an expression that made her spine tingle and which she had always been powerless to resist. She glanced round the vast room. 'I doubt it,' she replied.

'How did you get here?'

'By taxi.'

'Ah, well, in that case you'll be needing transport home, won't you?' Not giving her a chance to refuse, he took her arm and guided her gently but firmly from the floor. They said their goodbyes to Mr Rossington and Olive Jenkins, who by this time was delightfully light-headed, then, with Fiona vaguely aware of Marilyn Hughes's furious expression, they left the Gainsborough Room and made their way to Paul's silver-grey Rover in the hotel car park.

It was sheer madness; she knew that, but she seemed incapable of helping herself. The only thing that mattered was the fact that she was with him again, and even when he drew out of the car park and set off in the opposite direction to the Cathedral she did nothing to stop him.

There would be, she knew, time enough to count the cost of her folly later, but for the moment she just wanted him near her for a short time. With a little sigh she leaned her head back against the soft upholstery of the big car and luxuriated in the unaccustomed comfort. Then carefully she turned her head and stole a glance at Paul's profile. He was concentrating on the road ahead, but in the faint light from the dashboard and from her previous knowledge of him she could interpret his expression. There would be a faint frown between his brows and an intense look in the clear eyes, and she shivered slightly as she recalled those other times when she had known the intensity of that look.

Then as they drove through the silent streets she wondered briefly what his reaction would be if he were to discover the truth. Would he be angry? Angry that he hadn't been told of his son's existence? On the other hand, would he reject him, unable to face the responsibility? Whichever way, Fiona wasn't certain she could cope with the outcome, and thinking about it only made her all the more determined that he shouldn't know.

Almost as if he sensed her scrutiny, Paul glanced sideways at her, momentarily taking his eyes from the road, then he leaned across and covered her hands briefly with one of his.

Even at that point she could have stopped him, she knew that. She knew she should have stopped him, knew that she was simply making things more difficult for herself, but she did nothing. Even when she realised they were heading for the canal, where rumour had it the new registrar had an apartment in one of the old recently converted warehouses, she did nothing.

Only when he brought the car to a halt in front of the large dark outline of the warehouse did she speak.

'This isn't Cathedral Close,' she murmured wryly.

Paul rested his hands on the steering-wheel and turned towards her. Half of his face was in shadow, the rest illuminated by the light from an overhead street-lamp. 'I thought coffee might be in order before you go home—or maybe a nightcap?'

'Coffee will be fine, but it's very late, Paul.'

'I can make coffee very quickly.' He laughed, and, opening his door, he climbed out of the car.

Almost before Fiona had a chance to release her seat-belt he was round the car and had opened her door, helping her to alight almost as if he was afraid she would change her mind and demand to be taken home.

As if in a trance she followed him into his apartment, reason telling her that she was making a dreadful mistake, but at the same time the yearning to be with him overpowering her senses.

His apartment appeared to be one vast room on the first floor, divided into sections by differing floor levels. The walls were of soft mellow brickwork while huge arched windows opened on to iron balconies that overlooked the canal. The polished parquet flooring was covered by several skin rugs, and Oriental tapestries covered one wall. Beneath two windows on a raised dais was a king-sized bed with black and cream covers.

Fiona gazed round in astonishment and Paul grinned. 'You like it?'

'Yes, I do, very much, but how. . .?'

'Don't get too excited—it isn't mine. I'm renting it fully furnished from a guy I know who's into interior design. He's gone to the States for a year.'

'Well, it's certainly different.' Fiona let her gaze wander to the dining area, where a wrought-iron candle wheel was suspended from the ceiling above a round table.

'You can say that again! I was very lucky to get it. It's a far cry from hospital accommodation, isn't it?' He gave her a knowing look and she glanced quickly away, knowing he was referring to the tiny flat he'd had in Birmingham where they had spent so much time together. 'Why don't you take your coat off and make yourself comfortable? And I'll go and put the coffee on.'

He moved to the far side of the room behind a Chinese screen which no doubt housed the kitchen, and slowly Fiona slipped off her coat and sat down on the soft black leather sofa.

It was then that she felt a moment of panic. My God, what am I doing here? she thought as she gazed wildly around. Being alone with Paul Sheldon was the very thing she had been determined to avoid ever since he had walked back into her life, and here she was, not only alone with him, but in his apartment in the middle of the night. I must be mad, she thought, and had almost risen to her feet when he appeared with two pottery mugs of coffee, and, setting them down on a low table in front of the sofa, he sat down beside her.

He was silent for a moment, then, without looking at her, he said, 'All I can say is, it's about time.'

'What is?' She threw him a startled glance, and slowly he turned his head to look at her.

'That at last we have a chance to talk without being interrupted.'

'I did say, Paul, it's very late, and I have to get back. . .' She was silenced as he suddenly leaned across and, pulling her roughly into his arms, he brought his mouth down hard on hers.

The kiss seemed to go on forever, and while at first Fiona struggled, very soon long-forgotten sensations were rekindled by the touch of his lips and his hands, which quickly rendered her helpless with longing. When at last he pulled away it was merely to say, 'On second thoughts, who needs to talk when we have so much time to make up?'

The coffee forgotten, he lifted her up and carried her across the apartment to the dais beneath the high arched windows. Then with the silky black water below, the night sky above them and myriad lights from the city twinkling on the far bank of the canal, he gently lowered her on to the bed.

CHAPTER SIX

WHEN Paul had said that he thought what they had shared had been very special, he hadn't been exaggerating. Sex had always been very, very good between them, and the seven-year gap hadn't changed anything.

At first Fiona had been hesitant, unsure of herself, as he had lowered her on to the bed, then sat alongside her and gently pulled down the zip of her dress, slipping the silky material from her shoulders and revealing the silver-grey camisole she wore beneath. Then as he placed brief butterfly kisses along the line of her bare shoulder her last shred of resistance slipped away and she wound her arms around his neck.

For Fiona, at that moment, nothing else in the world mattered except that she was alone with the man she had always loved, and it seemed the most natural thing in the world that the evening should end like this. Against her better judgement she closed her mind to her previous decision to have nothing more to do with him, and as he undressed she lay back on the pillows and watched him.

The sight of him thrilled her now every bit as much as it had done all those years ago; his naked back as he sat on the edge of the bed, then, as he stood up and turned, the strength of his perfectly muscled physique, his lean thighs and well-shaped legs.

Then finally, as he stretched out beside her, taking her face and entangling his hands in her hair, she gave a little sigh before he brought his lips down fiercely on hers.

From that moment there was no halting the rush of their passion as memories mingled with present sensations, and if it had been Paul's intention to have a long leisurely arousal it was forgotten in the sudden urgency of the moment.

The intensity of Fiona's response shocked her, for it was as if she'd been simply waiting for this to happen, and when at last she surrendered to him the incredible sweetness of the moment had the quality of a homecoming after a long and arduous journey.

Her desire matched his in every way, their lovemaking as inevitable and spontaneous as the tide rushing to the shore, and after their passion exploded in a moment of mutual ecstasy she lay in his arms, satiated and utterly fulfilled.

For a long time they lay in silence, each absorbed in their own thoughts, Fiona knowing that later she would regret what had happened, but for the moment so intoxicated that she was content to let her thoughts drift in blissful limbo. Then, quite against her will, little niggling doubts crept in. Would Paul have noticed any difference in her? Would he have guessed that she'd had a child? Although she had regained her figure after Dominic's birth there could still be little telltale signs, and, after all, Paul was a doctor.

But he seemed not to have noticed anything unusual, and it was he who finally broke the silence, raising himself on one elbow and smiling down at her. 'Happy?' he murmured.

This was something he'd always said in the past after they'd made love, and she smiled and nodded.

'You know something?' Gently he traced a line down the side of her face. 'This must be like a good wine—the longer you keep it the better it gets. Mind you,' he leaned across and gazed deeply into her eyes, 'it bothers me when I think what we've been missing all this time.'

Fiona laughed softly. 'You can't tell me, Paul Sheldon, that you've been living the life of a monk, because I wouldn't believe you! Celibacy isn't a condition I associate with you.'

His eyes opened wide in an expression of injured innocence. 'Oh, how you misjudge me!' Sadly he shook his head, but there was a wicked gleam of amusement in his eyes. Then suddenly he grew serious and his expression changed, becoming intense again, and as he continued to caress the side of her face he said huskily, 'I won't deny anything, Fiona, I wouldn't insult your intelligence, but I can tell you one thing: I never completely got over you. You were always there at the back of my mind.' He paused, then, with what could have been a trace of anxiety, he asked, 'Is there a chance that you ever thought about me?'

She replied instantly without thinking, 'Oh, yes, Paul, you were often on my mind.' Then as she saw his expression change yet again she bit her lip, adding hastily, 'Of course, I've had other relationships too.'

'Oh, of course,' he added solemnly, and she threw him a suspicious glance, not convinced that he wasn't mocking her. 'There must have been other men in all that time,' he added seriously, 'but what you're saying is that none of them quite matched up to me, is that it?' He gave a wicked chuckle, and she threw a light punch at his chest.

'You're insufferable! All I meant was that a girl usually remembers her first love, and that's what you were, Paul.'

'First love. . .and dare I hope last love?' He stared at her, visibly holding his breath, waiting for her reply.

Fiona stirred uneasily. While they had been reliving the past and creating the present everything had seemed magical, but at the mention of shaping the future it was as if the spell was broken and she was reminded of the reality of the situation. But still he was waiting for a reply, and at last she said slowly, 'I don't know, Paul. . . I trusted you once, I'm not sure I could summon up that trust again. It took me a long time to get over you, and I know I couldn't cope with all that again.'

He sighed. 'I had no idea at the time that I was behaving so badly. I couldn't see beyond the fact that I had to get on career-wise. We were both young, and whereas you were probably ready to settle down I quite clearly wasn't. I also had no idea I'd hurt you so much, but it explains why you've been so hostile towards me since I arrived.'

She frowned. 'I wasn't aware I was being hostile.'

'Well, perhaps not hostile, maybe aloof would be a better word.'

'I just didn't want you to assume we could carry on where we left off, that's all. . .'

'And now that's precisely what's happened.' He smiled. 'But, Fiona, things are so different now. I'm not a struggling houseman any more, my prospects are good—what I'm asking you is to give me another chance. Will you do that?' As he was speaking he had moved his hand from her face under the black sheet that covered them and gently he cupped her breast, teasing and caressing with his strong fingers.

Immediately another shaft of desire surged through her veins, and helplessly she turned to him again.

'Paul. . . I really should be going home. . .' Her protest was smothered as his mouth found hers, and in the same moment he moved and his body covered hers again.

Much, much later Fiona stirred and, extricating herself from Paul's arms, she sat up and, leaning across him, tried to see his clock radio.

'What is it?' Sleepily he tried to pull her down into his arms again, but with a little gasp she successfully evaded his grasp and swung her legs out of the bed. Quickly she began to gather up her clothes from the floor where they had been abandoned in the frenzy of their reunion.

'Where are you going?'

She glanced over her shoulder and saw he had propped himself on one elbow and was watching her. His blond hair was delightfully tousled, giving him the little-boy appearance she had once loved so much. 'I have to get home. . .'

'Surely Lilli doesn't wait up for you? You're a big girl now.'

'It isn't that, Paul.'

'Then what?'

She hesitated, the pause barely perceptible as she sought for a suitable excuse, for she could hardly tell him the real problem, that her son would go into her room very early for a cuddle and would never understand why she wasn't there. At last she said, 'I always tell Lilli if I'm going to be late. Last night I said I didn't think I'd be much after midnight.'

'Even so. . .'

'Paul, it's nearly three o'clock! She'll be worrying if she's awake. I'm sorry, but I really do have to go. You needn't worry, I'll get a taxi.'

He gave a deep sigh. 'You'll do nothing of the sort.' Slowly he climbed out of bed and began to dress.

A soft drizzle was falling when they left the apartment a little later. Paul reversed the Rover to the entrance where Fiona was waiting.

The streets were silent and deserted, the damp pavements gleaming silver in the light from the overhead street-lamps, and as Paul drove through the night they were mostly silent. It wasn't until he turned in to the Close that he glanced sideways at Fiona and softly asked the inevitable question.

'Have you thought about what I asked?'

She sighed, and as he brought the big car to a halt she looked out of the window at the huge dark outline of the Cathedral that towered above them, comforting somehow by its very presence. 'I don't know, Paul,' she said at last. 'I really don't know.'

'If it's time you need, I'll give you time.' He leaned across and opened the door for her, at the same time gently kissing her. 'But don't take too long. I can assure you, after tonight, seeing you and working with you simply won't be enough.'

She stood in the doorway and watched him draw away, her thoughts and emotions a teeming mass of excitement and regret, longings and confusion, then with a sigh she turned and entered the silent house.

To her relief there was no sign of Lilli, and when she went upstairs there was no strip of light under her door. Quietly she opened Dominic's door and for several moments she stood by her son's bed watching him, then, bending down, she gently kissed the sleeping child and stole from the room.

The following morning, after Dominic had crept into her bed for his cuddle and she had showered and dressed, Fiona was joined in the kitchen by Lilli. Her questions appeared on the surface to be of only casual interest, but to Fiona, who knew her mother so well, they implied that she knew exactly what her daughter had been up to the previous night, and with whom.

She was glad to finally escape to work, only to find that there, if it were possible, life was even more difficult. The morning started predictably enough with an interrogation from Marilyn Hughes.

Fiona was in the utility-room at the time, checking supplies, and Marilyn came in to collect some sterile dressing packs for Mr Evans.

'So what happened to you last night?' she asked, raising her eyebrows.

'What do you mean?' Fiona knew exactly to what she was referring, but feigned innocence.

'Disappearing like that with Paul Sheldon. Did he take you home?' Marilyn demanded suspiciously, her dark eyes narrowing as she stared at Fiona.

Fiona nodded briefly, then, pointing to the dressings in Marilyn's hand, she said, 'I take it those are for Mr Evans?'

'What?' Marilyn glanced sharply at the packs. 'Yes, they are, but why should he have taken you home?'

'Who, Mr Evans?' Fiona laughed in an attempt to lighten the situation, but Marilyn was clearly upset. She obviously considered that because Paul had spent a good part of the evening with her it should have been her he had taken home.

She sighed impatiently, clearly irritated by Fiona's flippant attempt at humour. 'It seems to me that in the past you knew Paul Sheldon a darn sight better than you're letting on!'

Fiona turned, finally exasperated. 'And what if I did? Honestly, Marilyn, I really can't see that it's any of your business. Now, if you're ready I'll give you a hand with Mr Evans.'

Marilyn remained silent as they changed Mr Evans's dressings, and it was left to Fiona to chat to the patient.

'Your wounds are healing nicely, Jim,' she said after they had rolled him on to his side and removed his soiled dressings.

'There are two cuts, aren't there, Nurse?' he asked.

'Yes. One runs parallel to your spine, that's the longest one, and the other is to the side pointing towards your hip. That's where Mr Rossington took your bone graft.'

'I shall be glad when I can sit up,' he remarked, as Marilyn secured the fresh dressings with Micropore tape.

'I know,' said Fiona sympathetically. 'Three weeks' bed-rest must seem like a lifetime. Do you have plenty to read?'

'I find it difficult reading, lying so flat. But I don't mind too much, Nurse, not since my daughter brought me this personal stereo. It's passed many an hour, I can tell you.'

'Oh, that's good,' Fiona smiled as they rolled him on to his back again. 'What sort of music do you like?'

'Opera.' He smiled at the two nurses, but the

effort involved in changing his dressings had clearly tired him. 'I'm going to listen to *Carmen* now that you've done that.' He gave a sigh of relief and adjusted his ear-pieces.

'Rather him than me,' muttered Marilyn, as they pushed the dressings trolley away from his bed. 'I can't imagine anything worse than opera!'

'If it keeps him happy and occupied, it wouldn't matter if it was heavy metal,' remarked Fiona, then, leaving Marilyn, she hurried to the office to answer the phone.

It was the casualty officer who told her that they were sending a Mrs Emily Radforth up to the ward. She had had a fall at her home and X-rays had shown that she had fractured her femur. The casualty officer went on to say that Dr Sheldon would be along to see her shortly.

At the mention of Paul's name Fiona felt her heart leap. She hadn't seen him yet that day and she didn't know how she was going to act as if nothing had happened, especially with the eagle-eyed Marilyn, who would doubtless be watching her every move.

Mrs Radforth turned out to be a frail old lady of ninety who seemed terrified and bewildered by what had happened to her.

Fiona sat by her side and attempted to take her particulars, but this proved to be impossible as all the old lady seemed to be worrying about was whether anyone would feed her cat.

'You mustn't worry about your cat, Mrs Radforth,' Fiona said gently as she stroked the old lady's hand. 'We've had a word with a social worker and she'll take care of everything. She's going to let us know what arrangements she makes, and Tibby will be just fine. All you have to do is get better. Now, can you remember what happened exactly?'

Mrs Radforth stared up at Fiona and at first she shook her head, then, as Fiona waited patiently, the old lady gradually remembered what had happened to her.

'I was boiling a little bit of fish for Tibby's tea and I think the floor must have been wet, because I slipped up. Oh, dear!' She put one thin blue-veined hand to her face as something suddenly occurred to her.

'What is it, dear?'

'The gas—I never switched the gas off! My niece is always telling me off about that. . .'

'Well, you needn't worry about it this time,' replied Fiona firmly, 'because the ambulance men did it for you.' She glanced up as she finished speaking at the sound of footsteps, then her heart seemed to turn over again as her eyes met Paul's as he strode down the ward.

'I don't like doctors,' said Mrs Radforth, and her face creased up, partly with the pain she must have been experiencing and partly from anxiety. 'I haven't seen one for years,' she added.

'Well, I think you'll like this one,' replied Fiona wryly, as Paul reached the bed, and within moments had pulled up a stool and had exerted the full force of his charisma on Mrs Radforth.

Fiona stood quietly by, not interrupting, as Paul explained to the patient that they would be taking her down to the theatre a little later in the day after the effects of her breakfast had worn off; that they would be putting a pin and a plate in her leg to mend it; that she wouldn't know anything about it until she came round, when there would be some pain which they would control.

She watched, bemused, as he carefully examined the patient, his strong surgeon's hands gently summing up the extent of the damage. Only last night those same hands had caressed her, arousing her to the point of no return; now they were healing, reassuring. . . Almost as if he read her thoughts Paul looked up and their eyes met again in a precious moment of exclusion from the rest of the world, then, tearing his gaze away, he looked back at the patient.

'Now, Mrs Radforth, are you feeling a little happier about everything?'

'Oh, yes, yes, thank you, Doctor, much better. You see, I was so worried about my cat.'

'Your cat?' He raised his eyebrows and glanced enquiringly at Fiona. 'I trust that's all taken care of, Staff?'

Before Fiona had a chance to reply, the old lady said, 'Yes, Doctor, this nice nurse has arranged everything.' She sighed. 'You're all so kind in here, I'm just being a nuisance.'

'Not at all, Mrs Radforth, that's what we're here for.' Paul smiled, first for the patient, then for

Fiona as he left her to prepare the patient for her pre-med.

When she emerged from Mrs Radforth's cubicle Fiona was relieved to find that Paul had left the ward, no doubt to go back to the theatre. It disturbed her to have him working so close to her, especially on that particular morning.

She had slept very little when she eventually got to bed, for her brain had been teeming with the implications of what she had done. While part of her had known it was madness to go to Paul's apartment with what would inevitably follow, another part of her had longed to be with him again.

Now she was more confused than ever. Paul had made it very plain that he wanted to resume their relationship, but would he feel the same way when he knew all the facts? What would his reaction be when he found out that she had deliberately withheld the fact that he was the father of a six-year-old boy? And then on the other hand, even if he turned out to be delighted, did she want him in her life permanently? Could she trust him again, or would she be constantly afraid that he would break her heart for the second time?

And then again, there was Dominic himself to consider. How would he react to the sudden appearance of a father? He had had her to himself for so long that he might find it very difficult sharing her with another male.

And finally, for her part, Fiona was still unsure that she wanted any intrusion in her son's upbringing, for, as she had explained to Lilli, she had managed perfectly well on her own until now.

The questions had chased themselves round and round in her head for the remainder of the short night, leaving her exhausted but still curiously elated.

She spent the rest of the day trying to avoid Paul, afraid that he would demand a reply. She was just thinking she had succeeded and was preparing to go off duty when there was a knock on the office door, and her heart sank as he stepped into the room, closing the door behind him.

Without a word he came round the desk and took her into his arms, his lips hungrily seeking hers, stifling any protest she might have been about to make. Helplessly she felt her body's treacherous response and, giving up any attempt to stop him, allowed herself a brief moment of ecstasy.

Then as reason and reality slowly returned she pulled herself away from him, smoothing down her uniform and straightening her dishevelled hair as she tried to make light of the incident. 'Really, Dr Sheldon,' she said, conscious that her voice was husky, 'if Sister Buchanan should come in, I should think any chance of promotion I might have had would be ruined for all time!'

Paul laughed and caught hold of her hands. 'Have you finished your shift?' When she nodded he said, 'Good, I'll take you home.'

'No, Paul,' she said quickly—too quickly. 'That

is,' she added when she saw his questioning look of surprise, 'I want to walk home. Really, the exercise does me good, and it's a lovely day.' She glanced out of the office window as she spoke, where the late afternoon sunshine picked out the masses of daffodils in bloom in the hospital grounds.

He shrugged. 'As you wish, but I thought. . . I just thought that after last night. . .'

Tilting her head, she allowed her eyes to meet his. 'I know what you thought, Paul. I'm sorry, but you did agree to give me time, and that's what I need. I need time and space to think about what's happening.'

He stared at her for a long moment, then he nodded. 'All right, Fiona, I won't crowd you, I promise, but I'll tell you now, I don't intend to lose you now that I've found you again, and, I warn you, I don't think I'm capable of waiting for too long.'

Then he was gone, and she was left staring at the closed door. With a sigh she pressed her hands to her burning cheeks.

CHAPTER SEVEN

MUCH to Fiona's relief Lilli hadn't brought up the subject of Paul again, but this was probably due to the fact that her exhibition was looming on the horizon and all her energy was focused in that direction. Then one evening as Fiona was helping her to compile a catalogue of her paintings Paul's name suddenly came up.

It was very late, and both women had been working hard in the attic studio, and as Fiona suddenly stretched and yawned Lilli threw her an anxious glance.

'You look tired, darling,' she said.

'Do I?' Fiona ran her fingers through her blonde hair, then stood up with a sigh. 'Yes, I suppose I am tired. It's been pretty hectic at work just lately.'

Lilli hesitated, then said quietly, 'Talking of work, what about Paul?'

Fiona frowned. 'What about him?

'Well, if I remember rightly, the plan was to avoid him as much as possible. You haven't mentioned him again, and I just wondered how things were working out.'

'Oh, it isn't too bad,' Fiona replied, trying to sound as casual as she could while leaning over the workbench, apparently studying the catalogue, so that Lilli couldn't see her face.

When Lilli didn't answer she was finally forced to look up to find her mother staring at her with an expression on her face which seemed to say that Fiona hadn't fooled her one bit.

'Now tell the truth,' said Lilli softly.

Fiona turned away with a sharp movement that was almost one of anger, then she sighed and sat down again, resting her elbows on the bench and her chin in her hands. 'OK, so it's difficult, but I never imagined it was going to be easy when I settled for the third option,' she said with a wry smile.

'So does Paul know anything?' Lilli looked anxious again.

'About Dominic, you mean?' Fiona shook her head. 'Even if I hadn't made the decision, I know I'd find it extremely difficult to tell him.'

'I'm sure you would. After all, it isn't the sort of thing that comes up in casual conversation, is it?' Lilli gave a short laugh, then stood up and poured two mugs of coffee from the percolator which was always on the go in the studio. As the delicious aroma of the freshly ground coffee mingled with the pungent smell of turps and linseed oil, she turned slowly back to her daughter. 'You've been seeing him again, haven't you?' she asked quietly, handing her a mug.

'I. . . I. . .how. . .?' Fiona looked startled.

'How do I know?' Lilli raised her eyebrows. 'Mothers always know these things, Fe.'

They were silent for a few moments, each busy

with her own thoughts, then Lilli walked behind Fiona's chair and gently touched her shoulder.

'It puts a different slant on things, you know, darling.'

'What does?' Fiona looked up, startled.

'The fact that you're seeing each other again.'

'I don't see why. . .' Fiona began, then trailed off when she saw her mother's incredulous expression.

'Fe darling, you're being very naïve. I was dubious before about your decision not to have anything to do with Paul, but now. . .well, you must see how the situation has changed.' When Fiona remained silent, staring at the workbench, she continued, 'Have you thought, for example, what would happen if Paul found out from someone else? It wouldn't be too difficult—this town isn't that big, and you've already had one close shave when he brought you home the other day. . . Can you imagine what his reaction would be if he were to learn that sort of news from an outsider? No, I'm sorry, darling, but I think you have to reconsider.'

They were silent for a long moment, sipping their coffee, then Lilli leaned forward, pushing stray wisps of her hair, which still managed to look glamorous, behind her ears. 'How do you feel about him now?' The question was curious, but the look in her green eyes was one of concern.

Fiona slowly shook her head. 'I wish I knew.'

'Are you afraid of falling in love with him all over again?'

Fiona gave a short laugh. 'I'm not sure I ever fell out of love with him,' she replied, and there was no attempt to disguise the bitterness in her voice.

Lilli stared at her. 'Oh, darling, I had a feeling you'd loved him all this time. But you've allowed yourself to become bitter.'

'Do you blame me?' Fiona's head jerked up. 'It was him who left, not me!'

'I know. . . I know, but you must give yourself another chance. Does Paul know how you feel?'

Fiona shrugged, and Lilli continued, not giving her an opportunity to speak, 'You must tell him, Fe—you must!'

She stirred restlessly. 'How can I be sure I can trust him this time?'

'It'll be different now, I'm sure it will,' said Lilli, oblivious to the fact that she was almost echoing Paul's words. 'After all, there's Dominic now, and I can't see how Paul could fail to love him—he's so adorable.'

'But just supposing he didn't—love Dominic, I mean? Where would we be then? What do you suppose rejection like that would do to Dominic, or to me for that matter?' Angry unshed tears shone in Fiona's eyes as she faced her mother across the workbench.

'Well, I think you owe it to your son to give it a try—and, come to that, I think you owe it to yourself as well,' said Lilli firmly as she began clearing up her materials.

* * *

Lilli's words haunted Fiona the next morning as she hurried to work and sat through the report for the early shift. She had spent another restless night, muddled dreams of Paul and Dominic had dominated her few hours of sleep. The first light of morning had found her heavy-eyed and exhausted.

The report from the night staff suggested that they too had suffered a bad night, with two emergency admissions, difficult post-op care with Mrs Radforth and a pain-filled night for David Amery. Fiona had to make a conscious effort to switch off from her own problems and tune into her duties as acting sister. But as soon as she stepped out of the office on to the ward her personal life was forgotten as she was caught up in the fast pace of the morning ward routine.

Later she was helping one of the students with Mrs Radforth's bed bath when the old lady suddenly asked what the weather was like that day.

'Well, it's a bit chilly, but the sun is shining brightly,' replied Fiona, as she eased a fresh night-dress over the old lady's head.

'I shall be missing the flowers in my garden while I'm in here,' Mrs Radforth said ruefully, adding, 'All my daffodils were just coming out when I had my accident.'

Fiona straightened up and tried to see out of the window. 'It's a shame these windows are so high, otherwise you could see the lovely show of flowers in the hospital grounds. Kelly, please take particular care with those pressure-points,' she said quietly to the student who was assisting her, then as they finished making Mrs Radforth as comfort-able as possible she smiled down at the old lady. 'Now, is there anything else we can do for you?'

Mrs Radforth shook her head and smiled back. Since her admission, in spite of her pain she hadn't complained once, and now, freshly bathed and with her white hair neatly combed and held in place with a blue glass slide, she was propped up on her pillows for all the world like a queen waiting to hold an audience. 'No, thank you, Nurse, I don't think there's anything, unless you can bring the garden in here for me to see.'

Fiona laughed. 'Well, I don't think we can quite manage that, but I tell you what I can do. This weekend there's a spring fête in the hospital grounds, so in the afternoon I'll move your bed into the day-room so that you'll be able to watch what's going on.'

'Oh, thank you, Nurse. . .you're all so kind to me.' Mrs Radforth leaned back on to her pillows and closed her eyes.

As Fiona pulled back the curtains around the bed, out of the corner of her eye she saw that the consultants had entered the ward to do their round. Her heart jumped as it always did when she caught sight of Paul, then as she walked forward to meet them he smiled at her, and a feeling of such longing swept over her that she found it difficult to speak intelligently to Mr Rossington.

With every encounter with Paul she was finding

the situation more and more intolerable, and her recent talk with Lilli had made her realise that something would have to be done very soon. But still she dreaded the thought of telling him, and with each day she found herself delaying the task. For the moment, however, she had to concentrate on the job in hand, which that morning mainly involved David Amery.

To everyone's consternation he didn't appear to be showing many signs of improvement, and after much deliberation and studying of X-rays Mr Rossington decided to operate again.

'We'll take you down to Theatre again later today, David,' said the consultant. 'I'm not happy with your right leg, it looks as if the bone will have to be re-set.'

David only nodded in response, and as the surgeons moved away it was Fiona who caught the look of despair that crossed his features. She made a mental note to go back and chat to him when the ward round was over.

In the office she had further discussion with Mr Rossington and Paul about the other patients, their treatment and medication, then as they were leaving Stuart McVey arrived. He made some cheery quip to Paul to the effect that he was only waiting for Fiona to say when she would be going out with him, then he disappeared down the ward to see Mr Evans.

Fiona felt a blush tinge her cheeks and busied herself with some observation charts, unable to meet Paul's questioning gaze, then as he left the office he lightly touched her arm.

'Just don't forget who's first in the queue, will you?' he murmured softly, and for a brief moment he was so close that she felt his warm breath on the nape of her neck.

With a sigh she turned back to the ward and made her way to David's bedside. As usual he had his face turned to the wall, but as she approached he turned to look at her.

'I told you, didn't I?' he said bitterly, and she was struck afresh by the hopeless look in his eyes.

'Told me what?' She knew full well to what he was referring, but she pretended she didn't and tried to keep her tone light.

'That I'm going to be a useless cripple—well, all I can say is it's a good job me and Tracy have split up.' His breath caught in his throat and he swallowed and turned away again.

'I don't know where you've got the idea that you're going to be a cripple.'

'You heard what he said,' he retorted. 'That Mr Rossington, he said more surgery.'

'That's right,' replied Fiona calmly. 'That's exactly what I heard him say, but I certainly didn't hear the word cripple.'

'That's what he means, though, he just covers it all up in fancy talk. I wish he'd just come right out with it and tell me straight that my legs are useless now.'

'He won't tell you that, David, because it just isn't the truth. Mr Rossington is a very clever surgeon, and he's confident that he can get you back on your feet. . .the only trouble is, of course. . .' She hesitated.

'What?' He narrowed his eyes and looked up at her.

'Well, it's always easier in these cases if the patient is a fighter. . .'

'Who says I'm not?' David sounded indignant.

'No one. . .but—well, it doesn't seem to be coming over that you're fighting very hard. In fact,' Fiona lowered her voice and glanced over her shoulder to where Marilyn was adjusting another patient's traction weights, 'from where I'm standing it seems like you've given up.'

'That's rubbish!' David snorted. 'Of course I haven't given up!'

'In that case, why don't you let me give Tracy a ring and tell her she can come in and see you——'

'No!' he interrupted sharply. 'I don't want her here. . .besides, if I've got to go back for another op I shall be throwing up all over the place just like last time. I don't want anyone seeing me like that, not even my mum, OK?'

'All right, no one's going to make you do anything you don't want to,' replied Fiona. She returned to the office, feeling she really hadn't achieved anything and wishing that she could have somehow got David into a more optimistic frame of mind before he faced his next lot of surgery.

During her lunch break she met Jill, who was doing a few days on the orthopaedic outpatients' clinic, and the two of them made their way to the staff canteen.

'So what's new?' demanded Jill, as they carried their trays to their favourite window table. 'What have I missed?'

'Not a lot, really. A few new ones in the ward. Old Mrs Radforth's going on nicely; she's incredible for her age—oh, and David Amery's back to Theatre this afternoon, Henry R.'s going to have another go at his right leg.'

'Poor lad, how's he taking it?'

Fiona shook her head. 'Not very well. The trouble is he's so depressed; he's convinced he's going to end up in a wheelchair.'

'Has he made it up with his girlfriend?'

'No, and I'm sure that's half the trouble. . .still, I haven't given up in that quarter yet,' replied Fiona decisively as she tucked into her salad.

'Never known you as a matchmaker before.' Jill grinned and eyed her speculatively across the table.

Fiona shrugged. 'I'm not usually. . .it's just. . .well, I don't really know what it is. . .' She trailed off lamely.

'It couldn't by any chance have anything to do with the fact that you're feeling in a romantic frame of mind yourself?' Jill set her knife and fork down and with her head held to one side surveyed Fiona questioningly.

'I don't know what you're talking about,' Fiona replied sharply, but she was aware that her cheeks had grown hot.

'Oh, but I think you do. I'm not the only one to hear rumours about you and a certain dishy registrar.'

'What rumours?' Fiona demanded, then, suddenly aware that she had almost shouted the question, she glanced round at their colleagues dining at other tables, then deliberately lowering her voice she repeated, 'What rumours?'

'Oh, nothing much,' Jill replied airily as she stirred her coffee in a maddeningly slow way while Fiona waited impatiently. 'Only that the other night at Jenky's do this certain registrar danced the night away with a certain staff nurse, but at the end of the evening he took someone else home.'

'Oh, that! Don't you start,' muttered Fiona. 'I've already had the third degree about that from Marilyn.'

Jill grinned again and leaned closer. 'What did she say? I heard she was furious.'

Fiona shrugged. 'Well, she wasn't too happy, certainly, and she practically accused me of taking Paul away from her. I told her to mind her own business.'

'Good for you. . .now how about telling me what happened?' Fiona raised her eyebrows and Jill was forced to laugh aloud. 'I know—don't say it! Why don't I mind my own business as well! Sorry, Fiona, I thought you were going to tell me he's madly in love with you.'

'I should be so lucky!' Fiona answered lightly enough, but her heart was hammering as her friend skated so dangerously close to the truth. 'I have too many things on my mind at the moment for romantic involvements,' she ended.

'Like what?' Jill sounded slightly exasperated. She herself was engaged to an ambulance driver and she wanted everyone else to be as happy as she was.

'Well, Lilli has her exhibition coming up next week and I'm giving her as much help as I can with that.'

'That may be so, but you have yourself to think of as well,' said Jill firmly.

'I know that, but I have so much to be thankful for where Lilli's concerned, and I like to help her out whenever I can. She's done so much for Dominic and me.'

'Oh, talking of Dominic, you've just reminded me. Remember I told you about my nephews? Well, they're coming to stay this weekend. Would Dominic like to come out for the day with us tomorrow?'

'I'm sure he would, Jill, that's very kind of you. But will you be able to cope with three boys?'

'Oh, don't worry, Barry's coming with us.' Jill gave a slight shudder. 'I wouldn't tackle it alone.'

'Dominic has a judo lesson at the leisure centre first, but that should be over by ten o'clock.'

'Well, we'll pick him up from there. I thought perhaps we'd go to the adventure park and maybe McDonald's for lunch.'

'He'll love that,' Fiona smiled, and pushed her plate aside. 'And believe me, you've picked the right weekend, with Lilli being so busy and me on duty.'

Their lunch break over, the two girls returned to work, Jill to the afternoon outpatients' clinic and Fiona to the ward, where she found that Marilyn had given David his pre-med and prepared him for theatre. Marilyn had been very short with her since the night when Paul had taken her home, and Fiona couldn't help but wonder what her reaction would be if she knew the full story. She had made it quite obvious that she fancied her chances with the new registrar, openly playing up to him whenever the opportunity arose.

Fiona began her afternoon's work, dealing with two new admissions, both women, one a nurse with a history of severe back pain and the other for investigation of a painful elbow joint. The former was put on to immediate bed-rest and traction, while the latter was allowed to go to the day-room to watch the television as her treatment wouldn't begin until the following day.

This was followed by a long period of report-writing for Fiona, then she made her way to the store-room to check supplies. It was while she was stretching up to the top shelf to lift down some boxes of insulin syringes that she suddenly jumped as a pair of arms encircled her waist.

She stiffened and gave a cry, then Paul murmured softly against her hair, 'I hoped I might find you in here.' With a deft movement he kicked the door shut behind him, and for one reckless moment she leaned against him, thrilled as the

tremor that ran through his hard, lean body transferred itself to her. Dangerously he buried his face
in the hollow of her neck, at the same time
allowing his hands to roam lightly but urgently
over her body, her breasts, her waist and finally
coming to rest on her hips.

With a gasp she turned her face towards him,
powerless to resist in spite of the madness of their
situation, and for a brief moment of ecstasy his
mouth found hers, his tongue playing, gently
parting her lips, then her teeth, softly exploring
and arousing sensations of such sweet desire that
for a moment she would have thrown caution to
the winds and surrendered to him there behind
the store-room door.

It was the sudden clatter of a bedpan being
emptied in the sluice next door that brought them
both to their senses, and with a muffled groan
Paul pulled away from her.

'God, woman, have you any idea what you do
to me?' He stood back a pace and hungrily took in
every detail of her appearance, then with a tender
movement he leaned forward and straightened her
cap, which had come askew. 'Can't have the acting
sister going back on the ward in a state of disarray,
can we?' he chuckled.

Fiona grimaced. 'And what about the surgical
registrar? Isn't he supposed to be in Theatre this
afternoon? I can't imagine what this sort of thing
does to your operating ability.'

He grinned. 'It's incredible—the surge of adren-
alin works wonders!' He turned and opened the

door, then stood back, allowing her to leave the room first. As they stepped into the corridor the first person they saw was Marilyn Hughes as she came out of the sluice carrying the empty bedpan.

Her eyes narrowed suspiciously when she caught sight of them and she followed them back to the ward. Without another word Fiona went into the office to complete her order sheets and Paul went to speak to David, who by that time was being transferred on to a trolley by two porters.

A few minutes later Marilyn followed Fiona into the office. She still had the same accusing expression on her face and Fiona's attempts at light conversation were ignored. She had all but abandoned the attempt when Paul suddenly stuck his head round the office door.

'Are you two girls involved with this fête tomorrow afternoon?' he asked. His tone was easygoing and Fiona recognised his attempt to lighten the tension for Marilyn's benefit.

She smiled and shook her head. 'Afraid not, I'm on duty—some of us have to hold the fort, you know.'

Marilyn looked up sharply. 'Even if you were off duty, I doubt whether you'd have gone,' she said.

Paul frowned and looked puzzled. 'Oh? Fêtes not your scene? It is for the body-scanner appeal. . .'

'Oh, I dare say I would have done my bit——' Fiona began, then was silenced as Marilyn interrupted.

'Let's face it, Fiona, you have very little time for socialising, charity or otherwise.' She turned to Paul and, smiling sweetly up into his face, she explained, 'Fiona's a busy mum; she has a young son, and all her spare time is spent with him.'

CHAPTER EIGHT

THE silence in the office was almost tangible. Fiona remained perfectly still but was unable to look at Paul, while Marilyn, who doubtless considered that by maliciously imparting that choice piece of information she had furthered her chances with Paul, glanced triumphantly from one to the other. It was the sound of Paul's bleeper that finally, mercifully, broke the tense silence.

Fiona seemed incapable of either speech or action, and it was Marilyn who indicated for Paul to use the telephone. The silence continued as he dialled the number, and still Fiona was unable to meet his gaze.

'I'm needed in Theatre.' His voice was quiet and slightly husky. As he replaced the receiver she finally raised her eyes to his.

What she saw there was unfathomable; whether pain, accusation or surprise, she had no way of telling. Then he was gone, leaving her emotions in shatters and murder in her heart when she looked at Marilyn.

But she was given no further chance for speculation, as the phone rang almost immediately. As she reached out for the receiver her hand was shaking, and, even before she spoke, Marilyn, unaware of the extent of the havoc she had caused, left the room.

It was the casualty officer on the phone to say they were sending up a young girl who had been doing a paper round, had fallen from her bike and, putting out her hand to save herself, had fractured her clavicle.

Fiona glanced at her watch and saw that she still had another hour or so to get through before she could go off duty. Taking a deep breath, she made a determined effort to blot from her mind the events of the last few minutes, then, squaring her shoulders, she stepped out of the office to receive her new patient.

The girl, Lisa Woods, was more frightened than anything, and Fiona set about calming her down and reassuring her. Hers was probably only to be an overnight stay in the orthopaedic unit for observation. Her collarbone had been successfully attended to in Casualty, but there had been a high degree of shock. Her father was with her, but the girl was constantly asking for her mother.

'Will her mother be coming in?' Fiona asked Mr Woods.

He shook his head. 'I shouldn't think so—we're separated. She lives in Lanarkshire with her new boyfriend.' He glanced anxiously down at his white-faced daughter. 'Don't worry, love, everything will be all right. Lorna's coming in to see you when she finished work.'

'I don't want Lorna, I want Mummy,' replied Lisa tearfully.

Fiona turned away, but there was a niggle somewhere at the back of her mind, and it had something to do with how much children needed both
their parents. Hastily she dismissed the thought.
She couldn't allow herself to start thinking along
those lines now. Later she knew she wouldn't be
able to escape it, for all the old arguments would
come crowding back, and now everything had
changed, because Paul knew. She drew back the
curtains around Lisa's bed and a sick wave of fear
flooded over her. Oh, why had Marilyn said what
she had? She hadn't wanted Paul to learn of
Dominic's existence in that way. Desperately she
tried to thrust it from her mind again, but only
moments later it was back, and as she helped a
student nurse with Mr Evans's pressure-points she
found herself looking at her watch and wondering
how long Paul would be in Theatre.

She knew that this time it could be a long
operation for David and there was every chance
that her shift would end before it was over, so
there would be no opportunity to see Paul again
that day. Restlessly she went back to the office to
finish her reports, but she was unable to concentrate, and it was almost a relief when there came a
light tap on the door.

When she saw who it was, however, her heart
sank. David's girlfriend, Tracy Granger, stood
hesitantly in the open doorway.

'I'm sorry, Nurse, but I rang David's mum to see
how he was and she said he had to have another

operation. I had. . . I had to come.' Her voice wavered. 'I'm so worried about him. . .'

'Come in Tracy, and sit down,' said Fiona firmly, steeling herself yet again to switch off her own problems.

The girl closed the door behind her and, perching nervously on the edge of a chair, pushed back her long fair hair. 'Do you think. . .do you think I could see him. . .just for a few minutes?'

'No, Tracy, I'm sorry, but you can't.'

'I know he said he didn't want to see me, but. . .'

'It isn't that, Tracy.'

'What do you mean?' Fear flickered in the girl's bright blue eyes. 'What's happened to him?'

Fiona recognised the edge of hysteria in her voice and hastened to reassure her. 'Nothing's happened, Tracy. But he's still in Theatre. We're just waiting for him to come back.'

'Oh—oh, I see.' Tracy frowned. 'Why did he have to have another operation?'

'Because Mr Rossington—he's the surgeon— wasn't satisfied with the way David's leg was mending.'

'So what's he going to do?'

'Re-set it. Don't worry, Tracy, Mr Rossington is a very clever surgeon and what he's doing will be for the best.'

'Will David be able to walk again?' Tracy almost whispered the question.

'We sincerely hope so,' replied Fiona firmly.

'He thinks he'll end up in a wheelchair.' Tracy's

lip trembled again. 'That's why he's finished with me.'

'And how would you feel about that?' asked Fiona carefully.

'I wouldn't care. I love David, and, let's face it, if he was in a wheelchair he'd need someone to look after him, wouldn't he?'

'Hmm. I think that's what he's afraid of,' replied Fiona.'

'What do you mean? I don't understand.'

'David doesn't want you to be tied for the rest of your life.'

'But surely that's for me to decide?' cried Tracy.

'I agree,' replied Fiona calmly. 'And, having met you, I have no doubt that it would be what you would want—but I think we're all jumping the gun here. There's an excellent chance that David will make a full recovery.'

'But what do I do if he still refuses to see me?'

'Just give him time, Tracy, and let me have another talk to him.'

'When he comes back from the theatre, will he still be asleep?'

'Yes, I should think so.'

'Well, in that case, can I wait and see him? Please, Nurse! He won't even know I've been here, will he?' Tracy's eyes were suddenly shining, full of hope, as she looked at Fiona.

'Well. . .well, yes, I can't see why you shouldn't, but only for a few minutes, because the staff will be very busy with him.'

'You'll be here, won't you?' Tracy suddenly looked anxious again.

Fiona glanced at her watch and saw that her shift should have ended ten minutes earlier, then she glanced again at the face of the girl in front of her and smiled. 'Yes, I'll be here,' she replied. 'Now, if you'll wait, I'll go and see what's happening.'

As she left the office Fiona reflected that if she stayed on the ward until David returned at least she might stand a chance of seeing Paul when the team finished operating. Quite suddenly it had become imperative that she should see him before she went home.

She phoned down to the theatre from the telephone in the nurses' station so that Tracy wouldn't overhear what was said. The theatre sister told her that David was in the recovery unit and would soon be returning to the ward.

'Oh, there is just one other thing, Sister,' said Fiona before she replaced the receiver. 'Is Dr Sheldon still in theatre?'

'Yes, he is. We've just had an emergency admission and they're operating again.'

'I see—thank you.' She hung up. At least he was still in the building, she thought with a sigh of relief. Swiftly she returned to the office, where she told Tracy that David would shortly be arriving back on the ward. She then made her a cup of tea, drank one herself when she realised how badly she needed one, then returned to the ward, leaving Tracy sitting in the office with instructions to stay there until she came back for her. She didn't want the girl to see David before she had him settled and comfortable in bed.

A houseman accompanied David from the theatre and gave instructions for his medication. His was an open fracture, so he was to have a course of Cefradine, an antibiotic to combat any possible infection, along with Pethidine, a powerful analgesic, to control the pain. Also, as David would be immobile for such a long time, Mr Rossington had requested an anti-coagulant drug to prevent thrombosis, so the houseman wrote him up for a course of Heparin injections.

After the staff had set up his drip, secured the drainage tubes from his wounds and checked his blood-pressure, Fiona straightened his pillows, smoothed down his bedcovers and, with a final check on the sleeping patient, went to collect Tracy.

The girl looked even more frightened than she had before as she followed Fiona down the ward, and when finally she stepped through the curtains into the cubicle her eyes filled with tears as she looked down at the white-faced boy on the bed.

For a long time she simply stared at him, then slowly she reached out and gently lifted one of his hands from where it lay on the striped hospital bedcover.

Then she looked up at Fiona. 'Is he all right?' she whispered.

Fiona nodded. 'Mr Rossington is very optimistic,' she replied. 'Now, Tracy, we must leave him to rest.' Then as the girl turned to go, Fiona added, 'You could at least give him a kiss.'

Tracy coloured and leaned over and kissed him on the cheek, then, looking far happier than she had when she came in, she followed Fiona out of the ward.

At the door of the office she turned. 'Thank you, Nurse,' she said simply. 'Thank you for everything. I feel so much better now.'

'That's all right, Tracy. As I said earlier, I think you'll just have to give David time. Ring the ward whenever you like, write to him, and we'll see what happens.' Fiona watched the girl's retreating figure as she disappeared down the corridor, then with a sigh she went back into the office, her own problems surging once more to the surface.

A further phone call revealed that Paul had just left the theatre. Frantically Fiona re-dialled and asked to be put through to the medical secretaries' office. If anyone knew the whereabouts of the consultants it would be them.

Fortunately, Suzanne, Mr Rossington's secretary, answered and in reply to Fiona's query, she said, 'I'm sorry, Fiona, but Dr Sheldon isn't here.'

'Do you happen to know where he went when he came out of Theatre?'

'I'm sorry, I don't, but hold on a minute, Mr Rossington has just come in. I'll ask him.'

Anxiously Fiona gnawed the side of her thumb as she waited. He must be there. She had to talk to him. The time had now come to set the record straight. She jumped as Henry Rossington's voice suddenly boomed down the phone.

'Looking for Dr Sheldon, Staff Nurse? I'm afraid he isn't here. Is there anything I can do to help? Not about young Amery, is it?'

'Oh, no, Mr Rossington,' she replied hastily. 'Your patient is fine; it was another matter I needed to speak to Dr Sheldon about.'

'I see. Well, he did disappear pretty smartish— said something about giving an after-dinner speech at the university for an old friend of his father.'

'Thank you very much, Mr Rossington,' said Fiona, with a sinking feeling in her stomach. So she had missed him. He'd already gone, and by the sound of it he would be tied up for the rest of the evening if he was dining with Charles Farnsworth.

On her way home Fiona decided she would tell Lilli what had happened and ask her advice as to how she should handle it, but when she reached the house in the Close it was to find the place in uproar.

Lilli, working on the final painting for her exhibition, had forgotten the time until Jane had brought Dominic home from school. Consequently there was no dinner prepared. Dominic was in tears because he'd lost his PE kit at school and his teacher had told him he had to learn to be more responsible.

'What's responsible, Mum?' he asked Fiona, as she set to preparing vegetables for their evening meal, all thoughts of a cosy chat with Lilli now reluctantly abandoned.

'Well, in this case it means looking after yourself and your possessions,' she replied, looking down at her son, who was sitting at the kitchen table gazing solemnly up at her. She felt her throat constrict at the expression in his clear eyes. How often had she seen that same expression in the last few weeks in another pair of blue-grey eyes?

'But I did look after it,' he protested. 'I think someone's pinched it.'

'I'll ring Miss Simms on Monday and we'll try and get it sorted out. I expect someone's just taken it home by mistake. But it means your kit won't get washed this weekend.'

'My trainers were in there as well. I wanted those to wear to judo in the morning.'

'You'll just have to wear your play ones,' said Fiona. 'Oh, Dominic, I almost forgot—talking of judo, Jill will be picking you up after your lesson tomorrow.'

Dominic nodded. He knew Jill well and accepted the fact that sometimes other people helped out when Fiona was on duty. At his mother's next words, however, his face lit up with excitement.

'Jill has her nephews staying with her this weekend and she asked if you'd like to spend the day with them. She and Barry are taking them to the adventure park. I said I thought you'd like to go.'

'Oh, brill!' His eyes shone, the PE kit forgotten as he scrambled down from the table and rushed off to tell Lilli his news.

Throughout the long evening Fiona was on edge, certain that Paul would phone her when he returned from the university, but the telephone remained aggravatingly silent. Long after Dominic had gone to bed, while Lilli was still in her studio working, she sat alone agonising and trying to imagine what his reaction had been to Marilyn's bombshell. Had he suspected her child was his? In which case, did his silence now imply his anger with her for not telling him? Or, on the other hand, did he think her child was much younger, the result of another relationship? In that case, by now he was probably having serious doubts about her, imagining her to be promiscuous. At last she made up her mind. She would phone him at his flat and tell him she needed to speak to him.

She picked up the phone directory and flipped through the pages to the letter S. There were several Sheldons listed, but none with the initial P. Then she realised that he probably hadn't been in Merstonbury long enough to be listed and that the place would be in the name of its owner. Desperately she tried to remember if Paul had mentioned his friend's name. She knew he said he'd gone to the States for a year, but she couldn't recall whether or not he'd said his name.

Finally she went up to the studio, wondering if she dared ask Lilli to ring Charles Farnsworth's number at his rooms at the university on the chance that Paul was still there. Lilli, however, was so engrossed in her work that she hardly acknowledged her daughter's presence, so Fiona was reluctantly forced to accept that she couldn't contact Paul that night.

The following morning saw little change in tension in the Norris household. Fiona, having spent a bad night, was filled with anxiety about the day ahead, Dominic was so excited about his day out that he could hardly eat his breakfast, and Lilli seemed on the verge of a nervous breakdown because the finishing touches on her painting wouldn't go right. Eventually Fiona got ready for work, reminding Dominic that Jane and Neil would collect him and take him to the leisure centre for his judo lesson.

'OK,' he said, drinking his orange juice. 'I hope we don't have old Stinky Saunders this week.'

'I thought you said you had a new teacher,' said Fiona as she put on her jacket.

'We have, but he can't come every week.' Dominic slid down from the kitchen stool and, reaching up, gave his mother a kiss. ''Bye, Mum,' he said, then disappeared up the stairs to his room.

'Goodbye, Dominic—have a good time, won't you?' But he was gone, and with a pang Fiona gazed up the stairs, wishing it was herself that was taking her son out for the day. . .herself and Paul. . . Almost unbidden the thought darted into her mind, then she dismissed it and stepped out of the house into the bright spring sunshine.

It was usually quieter at the hospital at weekends, but this particular weekend was an exception, for when Fiona arrived it was to find that a large marquee had been erected in the grounds and various stalls and sideshows were being set up beneath the horse-chestnut trees.

The spring fête at St Catherine's was always a fun event, staged mainly by the medical students and student nurses to raise money for charity. This time, as Paul had reminded her, the money was to go towards a badly needed body-scanner. For a moment she half wished she was off duty so that she could help, but she was quickly caught up in the ward routine and she soon forgot the activities outside.

Somehow Fiona had been convinced that Paul would be on duty, and when she found that he wasn't she didn't know whether to be disappointed or relieved.

During the morning, as Fiona and Kelly were changing Emily Radforth's dressings, a message came up to the orthopaedic unit to say that a patient by the name of Simon Ziegler would be arriving the following day for a week's stay.

'Oh, it'll be nice to see Simon again,' said Fiona, and Kelly looked up curiously.

'Who is he?' she asked as she carefully disposed of the soiled dressings.

'Simon? Oh, he's a bit special on this ward. . .you could say he's our star patient,' replied Fiona. 'He's nineteen now, but two years ago he was involved in a bad skiing accident at Aviemore. He broke his neck, leaving him a quadraplegic. . .he was on this unit for a very long time. He comes back sometimes to give his mum a bit of a rest, but this time it seems she has to come into the Gynae unit to have a D and C, so Simon is going to stay with us.'

'Can he do anything for himself?' asked Kelly, taking the sterile dressings from their packet with forceps.

'Simon?' Fiona chuckled. 'You just wait and see!' She watched as the student completed the dressings, then she smiled down at the old lady. 'That's you sorted out for today, Emily. Are you feeling more comfy now?'

'Yes, thank you, dear.'

'And is there anything else you want?'

'Is it Saturday today?'

'It is.' Fiona smiled. 'And I haven't forgotten. I said we'd move you into the day-room later so that you can watch the fête, didn't I?'

Emily nodded, and looked quite excited at the prospect. As the two nurses moved away from her bed, Fiona said, 'We'll get as many as we can into the day-room; it'll do them good to have a change of scene.'

'Do you think David would like to go?' asked Kelly as she wheeled the dressing trolley into the sluice.

'Why don't you go and ask him when you've finished that?'

Fiona settled down to some paperwork, and a little later Kelly reported back that David said he wasn't interested in seeing the fête.

Fiona sighed. 'Oh, well. . .we tried, but maybe he's still feeling groggy after his op. Never mind, we'll wheel Jim Evans's bed down there. I'm sure he'd like a change of scenery; he must know every crack in the ceiling above his bed by now.'

'When will he be getting out of bed?' asked Kelly.

Fiona glanced at a chart of progress reports on the office wall. 'Early next week, providing we get the OK from Mr Rossington and Stuart McVey, who'll be responsible for getting him walking again.'

As lunchtime approached Fiona found herself finding excuses to go into the day-room to look out of the window. She had a feeling that after his remarks of the previous day Paul might be helping with the fête, but by the time she went to lunch there was still no sign of him either on the ward or in the grounds.

She took her lunch alone and was pleased for the brief solitary respite, using it to try to plan what she would say to him when eventually she saw him again. Ever since Marilyn had told him about Dominic, Fiona had had a sneaking suspicion that Paul was deliberately avoiding her, and she knew she wouldn't rest until she had seen him and had a chance to explain. How he took her explanation was another matter entirely.

On her return to the ward the first thing she did was to carry out her promise to Emily Radforth and wheel her bed into the day-room. The old lady exclaimed with delight at the activity in the grounds, which were beginning to fill up now with members of the public, who swarmed around the stalls and sideshows. Then Fiona went down to

the men's ward and with Kelly's help she pushed
Jim Evans's bed right through the two wards so
that he too could watch the fun. As she passed
David's bed she glanced at him, but he had his
eyes closed, seemingly asleep and oblivious to
what was going on around him. She sighed,
inwardly resolving that she would try to spend
some time with him in the next few days and
attempt to lift him out of his depression.

Fiona spent a short while in the day-room with
her patients, the two in their beds and the dozen
or so who were mobile and were sitting in chairs
facing the big picture windows. When the
Saturday afternoon visitors arrived, however, the
day-room began to get a bit crowded, so with a
last glance out of the window she returned to her
office.

It was about half an hour later that she had a
visit from Sister Buchanan, who was officially off
duty.

'Hello, couldn't you stay away?' Fiona looked
up from the desk with a smile.

'I came in for the fête,' replied Audrey Buchanan.
'But I thought perhaps you might like a look
round. There are some nice things on the stalls,
and if you don't go now the best will be gone.'

'That's kind of you—thanks, I would like to
have a look.' Fiona stood up and, handing over
the keys to the drug cupboard, she said, 'I won't
be long.'

'Oh, take your time,' said Audrey with a laugh.

'My feet are killing me! I'm glad to sit down for five minutes.'

She saw him almost as soon as she stepped out of the door. He was standing beside the tombola stall, obviously helping Henry Rossington to drum up custom. For once the white coat and immaculate suit were missing and in their place he looked casual and very handsome in denims and a sweatshirt. His hair shone in the bright sunlight, and as he suddenly looked up and saw her she felt her heart miss a beat.

Slowly she began to walk towards him across the short grass, desperate to talk to him but at the same time fearful of his reaction. He watched her all the time, but then when she had almost reached him she suddenly realised that he was no longer looking at her but at a point in the distance over her shoulder.

Some instinct made her turn, and what she saw brought a gasp to her lips. Dominic was running towards her across the grass, a broad smile on his face, his arms outstretched. Behind him came two other little boys, and some way behind them she was vaguely aware of Jill and Barry.

Somehow she managed to open her arms to welcome her son, but as he reached her he suddenly stopped and dropped his arms to his sides.

'Dominic. . .?' She stared at him, puzzled, and slowly it dawned on her that the broad grin on his face wasn't for her but for the man behind her.

Startled, she looked quickly at Paul and saw the same grin on his face. 'Hello, Dominic,' he said.

Speechlessly Fiona looked back at her son. 'Hello,' he replied, then, looking up at Fiona, he whispered, 'That's him, Mum—Mr Sheldon. He's my new judo teacher.'

CHAPTER NINE

AT FIRST Fiona was only able to stare at Dominic in amazement, then before she had time to come to her senses the other two boys and Jill and Barry had joined them.

'Hi, Fiona, we thought we'd bring the boys in to see the fête and we wanted to ask you if Dominic could stay the night.'

'Well. . .' Fiona hesitated.

'Please, Mum, please let me!' Dominic tugged at her sleeve.

'We're going to have a barbecue,' Jill went on to explain, 'and it may go on a bit late. Have you finished your shift yet?'

Fiona shook her head, unable to bring herself to look at Paul. 'No, not yet,' she replied weakly. 'Sister let me come out to see what was going on.'

'Well, we'll let the boys enjoy themselves for a while—they want to have a go on Spin a Wheel. . .'

'Then can I go home with them?' pleaded Dominic again.

'I suppose so, if Jill really hasn't had enough.'

'No, Mum, she hasn't,' said Dominic, throwing Jill an anxious glance. 'We've had a super day; we went to the adventure park, then to McDonald's for burger and chips.'

'I'm glad you've enjoyed yourselves.' Fiona turned to Jill, but out of the corner of her eye she noticed that Paul had turned and was watching Dominic as he ran off with the other boys towards the sideshows. 'Thanks a lot, Jill. I can see that Dominic's had a wonderful time,' she said.

'We'll pick up his night things from Lilli on the way home,' said Jill with a smile, then with a wave she hurried off to join Barry and the boys as they headed for the sideshows.

'I suppose I'd better be getting back,' said Fiona to no one in particular.

'But you haven't seen the stalls yet,' said Paul softly. He had moved quietly behind her and was standing very close.

'I don't think I want to bother any more,' she replied.

'Nonsense, of course you must. Come on, I'll walk round with you.' With a nod in Henry Rossington's direction he took her elbow and firmly moved her away from the tombola stall.

There was an impressive display of handicrafts, books, cakes and confectionery on the stalls, and at any other time Fiona would have been quite happy to spend time browsing, but after what had just happened she found herself walking round in a daze, oblivious to what was on show.

It had come as a tremendous shock to her to find out that Dominic and Paul had actually met—and not only met but that they seemed to be on the best of terms. Once she glanced tentatively at Paul's face, but his expression was set and gave away nothing of his feelings. Her mind in a whirl, she desperately tried to sort out the facts. For a start Paul now knew that she had a son. Had he by now put two and two together and realised that Dominic was his? Had he seen the likeness to himself in the little boy he had been taking for judo lessons, and, if he had, when had he seen it?

The questions chased themselves round and round in her mind as she miserably trailed round the stalls after Paul, then he paused at one stall and bought a bag of home-made chocolate fudge, handing it to her with a grin.

'You always did like chocolate fudge, didn't you?' he said.

Whether it was the reference to their past relationship or the fact that there was a sudden chill in the air reminding them that it was getting late Fiona didn't know, but quite suddenly something prompted him to lean closer to her and, taking her chin in his hand he tilted her face, forcing her to look into his eyes.

'Fe,' he said using Lilli's pet name for her, 'we have to talk.'

She nodded and sighed. 'Yes, Paul, I know.'

He glanced at his watch. 'How long before you come off duty?'

'About an hour.'

'Right, I'll wait for you and take you home.'

She hesitated, then shrugged. It made no difference now if he took her home. He knew about Dominic and she no longer had anything to hide.

Fiona wasn't sure how she got through the next

hour, but somehow she managed to return to the ward and complete her shift.

Both Jim Evans and Emily Radforth were delighted with their spell in the day-room watching the proceedings in the grounds, and while Fiona took them back to the ward they talked incessantly about all they had seen.

And then at last, after what seemed like eternity, her shift was over. She handed over to another staff nurse and left the hospital, to find Paul waiting for her in the car park in his Rover.

She had been trying to rehearse what she was going to say to him, but when she got into the car and he drew away out of the hospital car park into the evening traffic she found she couldn't put anything into words. Finally it was Paul who broke the silence, but even then it wasn't until he drew into Cathedral Close.

'Are you going to ask me in this time?' he said, and when she didn't immediately reply he added, 'Isn't it about time I said a proper hello to Lilli?'

As they stepped from the car Lilli opened the front door.

'Fiona! Paul!' She smiled, as if it was the most natural thing in the world for them to be together. 'Do come in! I only wish I could stay and talk to you both, but I'm meeting Charles for dinner—ah, here's my taxi now!' she exclaimed, as a black cab pulled up behind Paul's car. 'Goodbye, darlings, there's plenty of food in the fridge and a bottle of wine, so help yourselves.' With a wave of her hand she was gone.

Fiona turned to Paul and pulled a face. He raised his eyebrows in response, then followed her into the tiny terraced house and closed the door behind him.

She prepared a light meal for them both, putting the wine to chill as she did so, then as she carried the tray through to the dining alcove that overlooked the garden she noticed that Paul had picked up a framed photograph from the mantelpiece and was studying it intently. It was a picture of Dominic taken when he was three years old. As she set the tray down Paul turned, and her eyes met his.

But it wasn't until after they had eaten and were lingering over their wine, watching the last of the evening twilight as it deepened into darkness, that he asked the inevitable question. By that time Fiona had had time to compose herself and felt quite calm.

'He's a fine boy,' said Paul without looking at her.

'Yes, he is,' she replied softly, turning her head slightly to look at the photograph which he had replaced on the mantelpiece.

'Just one question, Fiona.' Carefully he twirled the stem of his wine glass, apparently intently inspecting the fine cut of Lilli's lead crystal.

'Of course,' she replied with a small sigh.

'How soon after I left did you know?'

She hesitated, then slowly she said, 'I suspected before you left. . .'

Paul set down the glass carefully and stared at her. 'Then why didn't you——'

'Say anything?' she interrupted quickly, and when he nodded she shrugged slightly and turned her face away. 'I'm not entirely sure, Paul. It was a very long time ago and I believe my motives may have since become distorted in my mind.'

'Try and remember,' he said.

She sighed reflectively, then very slowly she tried to recall the past and how she had felt when she had learnt she was pregnant. 'At first I was horrified—after all, it wasn't exactly planned, was it?'

He shook his head. 'That's true. I still don't understand how it happened. . .we were always so careful.'

'It was when I changed the brand of pill I was taking—we should apparently have taken extra precautions during that time.'

'I didn't even know you had changed brands.'

'I know you didn't. It was my fault, I should have taken more care.'

'Do you know, it never even occurred to me to ask questions. As far as I was concerned you were on the Pill and I had nothing further to worry about. My God, the arrogance of youth! But. . .surely I wasn't such a chauvinistic pig that you couldn't have told me?'

'Oh, Paul, no. It wasn't like that, honestly.' Fiona stared at him helplessly, suddenly at a loss as to how she was going to make him understand, then slowly it dawned on her that all she could do was to tell him the truth. 'You see. . .' she faltered, 'I loved you so very much, and when you left I was convinced you'd stopped loving me. I thought that if I told you about the baby you'd think I'd tricked you into staying. I suppose also my pride came into it, because I didn't want you to stay with me just because of the baby.'

For a long time he stared at her across the table, then with a deep sigh he leaned his head back and closed his eyes. 'Oh, Fiona,' was all he said.

There was a long silence between them, then finally it was Fiona who spoke. 'What would you have done, Paul?'

He opened his eyes. 'I can't tell you after all these years exactly what my reaction would have been, but I'm pretty certain I would have stayed with you.'

'Because of the baby?'

'I suppose so. . .but not only because of the baby. My God, Fe, you're making me sound like some sort of monster! I loved you too, you know. I only cooled things because of my career—I told you that. I had my parents breathing down my neck at the time as well. They'd made a lot of sacrifices to put me through medical school and I didn't feel I should be thinking about marriage so soon. But I also imagined at the time that we'd keep in touch and that our relationship would have continued, but when you didn't answer my letters I assumed you didn't want to know any more.'

'And now? How do you feel now?' Fiona held her breath as he stood up and, resting his hands on the table, stared down at her.

'I'm having difficulty analysing my feelings now. . . I suppose I'm angry with you for not telling me. I bitterly regret the years that have been wasted. . .the years that I had a son growing up and knew nothing about it, and then. . .then I look at you and I know I want you as much now as I did then.'

In an instant he was round the table and half lifting her to her feet, his arms around her. With a sigh she leaned against him, the pent-up tension slowly ebbing away, then as she lifted her face to his and his lips found hers she felt the familiar surge of desire as her body's chemistry responded to his. Decisively he led her to the floral-patterned sofa and drew her down so that she lay half across him with her head resting on his chest. For a long time they lay in silence, perfectly content with each other's company, then, tilting her head back, Fiona looked up at him.

'Where do we go from here, Paul?' she asked softly.

'How about the bedroom?' The old glint of amusement was back in his eyes, and she was forced to laugh.

'That wasn't what I meant,' she protested.

'Pity, because it's certainly what I'd like,' he replied, allowing his hand to cup her breast while he buried his face in the vulnerable hollow of her neck.

'Well, that's quite out of the question,' she replied, drawing her breath in sharply as his hands became more adventurous. 'Lilli and Charles could come back at any time.'

'And you think they'd disapprove?' He raised his head and looked into her eyes. 'They'd probably be envious.'

'Paul! That's my mother you're talking about!'

He grinned, moving his hand to her thigh, gently but firmly caressing with rhythmic movements. 'I know, but, let's face it, Lilli's not like most mothers, is she?'

'No, I suppose not, but you're getting off the subject. What I meant when I said where do we go from here was what are we going to do, about us and Dominic?'

'I think we should take things very slowly. . .one day at a time. I don't want to rush you or Dominic, but I think you know what I want, Fiona.' As he was speaking Paul drew his hand up the front of her leg, and as she felt the hardening of his body beneath her she felt the automatic ache deep inside her own body as her longing for him intensified. 'I don't think we should tell Dominic at this point who I am, but I would like the opportunity of getting to know him better, if I may. In fact. . .' he hesitated '. . .I think the best thing all round would be a period of getting to know each other again. What do you think?'

She nodded. 'Yes, Paul, that seems like a good idea.'

'So what are you doing tomorrow?'

She laughed. 'I thought you said not to rush things!'

'I also said I regretted all the time we'd wasted. As far as I'm concerned, we have a hell of a lot of time to make up, so how about tomorrow?'

'Well, I'm on duty until one o'clock, then I usually take Dominic out on Sunday afternoons.'

'Do you think he'd mind if I tagged along?'

'I'm sure he wouldn't. He seems pretty keen on you, anyway, seeing you're his judo teacher.'

'I'm pleased you sent him for judo lessons, Fiona.'

She shrugged. 'It was something I always remembered, how you used to say that all little boys should be taught self-defence.'

'Or little girls, for that matter.' Paul smiled as he tightened his grip around her, imprisoning her against him. 'Just think, if you'd learnt self-defence you could have got away from me by now.'

'Who says I want to get away?'

Then, when his actions became more urgent, she again laughingly protested, saying they couldn't go up to the bedroom in case Lilli returned.

He replied, 'Who said anything about the bedroom? I'm quite happy to stay on the sofa for what I have in mind, but I want you to promise me one thing.'

Fiona raised her eyebrows and he continued, 'Tomorrow evening, after we've brought Dominic home, will Lilli look after him?'

'I should think so.'

He sighed. 'Good. In that case I'd like to take you to dinner, then we can go back to my apartment, where we can accomplish anything we can't quite manage on this sofa!'

The following morning when Fiona left for work her spirits were higher than they had been for weeks, but she found herself incapable of analysing her feelings, for she hardly dared to hope that everything was going to work out for the best. Reason told her that it could never be that simple, as she had explained to Lilli the night before when the two of them had sat drinking coffee far into the night.

'There are two issues here that you mustn't lose sight of,' Lilli had said. 'One is that you still love Paul and the other is that he seems to feel the same way about you. And really, darling, at the end of the day that's all that matters.'

'Oh, Lilli, you really are the most incurable romantic,' Fiona had said with a laugh, then, growing serious, she had added, 'But of course the other issue is still Dominic.'

'Well, by the sound of things it looks as if you're halfway there with that as well. At least they've met, and Dominic appears to like Paul, but wasn't that an incredible coincidence over the judo lessons?'

Fiona had agreed that yes, it was, and it was that thought that kept creeping into her mind on her way to work, but as usual as soon as she set foot on the ward all personal thoughts were pushed to the back of her mind as the needs of her patients claimed every ounce of her attention.

The highlight of the morning was the arrival of Simon Ziegler on the ward. He was greeted with pleasure and affection from those members of staff who remembered his fierce battle, and with curiosity by those who had heard about him and the measure of independence he had achieved. As Fiona wheeled him down the ward he bombarded her with stories of his latest exploits with the many computerised gadgets he'd had installed in his home, then when she had got him settled in his bed he presented her with a painting he had done by manoeuvring the paintbrush with his mouth.

'Oh, Simon, it's lovely!' she exclaimed, as she carefully examined the winter's scene he had so delicately depicted. 'I'll take it and show it to my mother, then we must talk again about you exhibiting some of your paintings.'

By the middle of the morning Simon had become the life and soul of the ward, and his cheerful optimistic approach to his handicap had spread to staff and patients alike.

Shortly before noon, Paul appeared unexpectedly on the ward. Fiona looked up in surprise from the report she was writing to find him standing in the open doorway of the office.

'Hello,' she said, and the delight must have been only too obvious in her tone. 'I wasn't expecting to see you this morning.'

'I couldn't stay away.' He grinned, his hand on his heart as he spoke. Then more seriously, he added, 'Actually, I'm not on duty, but I called in to see David Amery—apparently he had a bad night.'

Fiona nodded and handed him the night sister's report, then as he read it she took the opportunity to watch him unobserved, and, as she studied his strong features, the fair complexion and blue-grey eyes, her heart melted. Briefly she allowed her gaze to wander to his hands as they lightly held the sheaf of papers. They were so beautifully shaped that they could have belonged to an artist or a musician, but she knew the strength that was combined with the sensitivity, the strength required in the hands of a surgeon.

'Hmmm,' he said thoughtfully, handing her back the report. 'He really isn't too good, is he?'

'No, and depression still seems to be his main problem,' she replied.

'I thought he'd have got over that by now, but it rather looks as if we'll have to start treating it.' He paused reflectively, walking to the window and looking out at the spring flowers in the grounds below. 'I think I'll go and have a chat with him, if that's OK?'

'Of course.' She stood up, replacing the cap on her pen. 'I'll come through with you.'

As they reached the office door Paul again glanced back at the window. 'At least we've got a nice day to take Dominic out. He told me he has a dragon kite—suppose we take it on to the Common?'

Fiona smiled and nodded, but as they left the office and walked down the ward to David's bed she found herself wondering just how many other things Paul knew about Dominic.

David had his eyes closed as they approached his bed, but when they stopped he opened them, looking suspiciously at Fiona.

'Not another injection!' he exclaimed.

Fiona shook her head and explained to Paul that David's course of Heparin injections to prevent his blood clotting were proving painful and causing bruising.

'No, David,' said Paul with a laugh as he drew up a stool alongside the bed, 'we haven't come to stick any more needles into you. In fact, I've only really come for a chat.'

'I'll leave you to it and go and see Simon,' said Fiona, turning away, then she paused as David suddenly called her back.

'What happened to him?' he asked curiously, nodding in the direction of Simon's bed. His curtains were drawn, but sounds of laughter and light-hearted banter could be heard between him and the nurses who were attending to him.

'He was involved in a bad skiing accident,' explained Fiona. 'He broke his neck.'

'Good God! How awful!' David hesitated and Fiona watched him as he digested the information, then he looked up at her again. 'How old is he?' he asked slowly.

'Nineteen,' replied Fiona.

'That's dreadful. . . Can't he move at all?'

'Only his head.' It was Paul who answered this time.

'Imagine that happening. . .and at nineteen. . .'
David shook his head, as if contemplating the
horror of the possibility.

'Oh, it hasn't just happened,' said Fiona swiftly.
'It was two years ago, when he was on holiday at
Aviemore.'

In the silence that followed David gaped at her.
'You mean he's been like that for two years?'

Fiona nodded, and Paul said, 'He has, but even
worse than that is the fact that he'll be like it for
the rest of his life.' He glanced at David's stricken
expression, then allowed his gaze to flicker to
Fiona.

Her eyes met his for a fraction of a second as
they read each other's thoughts, then Fiona moved
away, leaving Paul to chat to his patient.

Half an hour later, while the patients were
eating their lunch, Paul joined Fiona in the office.

'Did you get anywhere with David?' she asked
hopefully.

'I'm not certain that I actually did much good,
but I think young Simon's presence in the ward
might have helped.'

'I wondered if it would. It so often happens
when someone thinks the end of the world has
come, that they see someone worse off than themselves. I'll certainly encourage Simon to talk to
David.'

Paul glanced at his watch. 'I have to go up to my
office for a bit, then I might as well wait until you
finish your shift so we can go together and pick up
Dominic,' he said. He had spoken quietly, but

when Fiona looked up she saw that Marilyn was standing at the linen cupboard outside the office and, judging by the expression on her face, had heard what Paul had said.

As he disappeared down the corridor, she looked accusingly at Fiona. 'Are you two going out together?' she asked bluntly.

'I suppose you could say that,' Fiona replied casually.

Marilyn sniffed, then looked down her nose at Fiona, her expression implying that she didn't know what he saw in her, and suddenly Fiona was goaded into retaliation.

'You know something, Marilyn? I think it has something to do with the fact that I have a son. . .you see, Paul loves kids.'

As Marilyn flounced off down the ward, Fiona watched her go, trying to suppress her laughter. After all, Marilyn had obviously been convinced that the fact that Fiona had a son would put Paul off, but as she turned back into the office Fiona found her own words ringing in her ears and momentarily she shivered. Could it be that it was only Dominic whom Paul wanted?

CHAPTER TEN

THEY picked up Dominic in Paul's car and drove to the wide open area of heathland high above the town. It was a bright sunny afternoon and the clear blue sky was dotted with ragged clouds chased by a keen breeze. Perfect conditions for flying a kite.

As soon as they parked, Dominic scrambled from the back seat of the car, tugging his dragon-shaped kite behind him, and Fiona smiled as she watched him set off across the short springy turf. He hadn't questioned the fact that they were going out with Paul, taking it in his stride almost as if he'd expected it.

Paul smiled at her across the roof of the car as he locked the door. 'Now comes the test as to whether or not I'm fit,' he said, pulling a face. Leaving her to follow more slowly, he set off at a steady run after Dominic.

For once Fiona was content to let someone else keep up with Dominic, because usually it was herself who had to run with him, join in his games and generally play the role of mother and father. With a rare feeling of perfect contentment, she strolled across the Common, feeling the sun on her face as the breeze caught at her hair, whipping tendrils across her cheeks.

146

It was a sudden shout from Dominic that made her stop, and with one hand shielding her eyes against the strong sunlight she watched as the dragon kite, brightly coloured in shades of scarlet and blue, soared high above them, dipping and turning as it climbed.

As she caught up with them she smiled to see that Paul was controlling the strings, while Dominic jumped excitedly up and down, clapping his hands.

'Look, Mum, look how high it is! We've never got it that high before, have we? Mr Sheldon says the weather's just right today.'

'It's super, Dominic,' agreed Fiona, then, with a quick glance at the back of Paul's head, she added, 'and it's Dr Sheldon, Dominic, not Mr Sheldon.'

Paul turned his head for a moment, taking his eyes off the kite. 'Oh, I think we can do away with all that. Dominic can call me Paul. . .at least for the time being,' he added as he caught Fiona's eye.

Before she had a chance to reply there came a sudden squeal from Dominic. 'Oh, look, look—it's coming down!'

Paul hastily turned back to the job in hand and Fiona wandered off towards a group of large rocks that looked as if they might provide shelter from the keen wind.

She sat down on the rough grass and rested her back against the rock face. Far below her sprawled the city, neat rows of slate-roofed houses, the new shopping precinct and the old buildings of the hospital and university. The sun glinted on the spires of the Cathedral and several churches and on the canal which looked like a long silver ribbon stretching into the distance. She had come to love the old cathedral city in the two years since she had been there, and when the question of her leaving had arisen she had been horrified. Now it rather seemed as if she could dismiss that fear, and for the umpteenth time she found herself wondering if she could dare to hope that everything would turn out for the best.

Almost as if he could read her thoughts, Paul suddenly dropped down beside her, gasping for breath after running the length of the Common with the kite.

'I guess I'm just not that fit,' he puffed, clutching his chest in mock agony.

'Where's Dominic?' Fiona turned her head, then caught a glimpse of her son's royal blue tracksuit as he scrambled about on the rocks behind them.

'I wish I had a quarter of his energy,' said Paul wryly.

'I know,' Fiona laughed. 'He never stops; he's on the go from morning till night.'

They were silent for a moment, staring down at the scene below them, then quietly Paul said, 'He's a credit to you, Fiona. You've done a wonderful job with him.'

She shrugged. 'I've done my best.'

'It can't have been easy.' Paul linked his hands between his knees and turned his head to look at her.

'We've had our rough patches,' she admitted, then added, 'but Lilli's been marvellous.'

'I can imagine. She's one in a million. I must remember to thank her some time for all she's done for my son.'

At his words Fiona jerked her head up sharply to make certain that Dominic wasn't in earshot. It still seemed strange to hear Paul talk in this fashion. 'You make it sound as if Lilli won't be doing any more for him,' she said.

'Well, it does sound as if she's done enough,' he replied firmly. 'And after all, she does have her own life to lead.'

'Oh, I don't know—she's got so used to having Dominic around that I think she'd be quite lost without him.'

Paul turned his head again to look at her. 'Have you been going around with your eyes closed lately?'

'What do you mean?' she demanded indignantly.

'I mean where Lilli's concerned, or at least where Lilli and Charles are concerned.'

Fiona remained silent, knowing that she had been unwilling to face up to what was happening between her mother and the handsome don from the university.

'She's entitled to her happiness, and from what I've heard Charles thinks the world of her.'

'I know,' Fiona stirred restlessly, 'and I'd be the last one to deny her that happiness, especially after all she's done for us. . .but. . .' She trailed off as Dominic suddenly appeared on the ledge of rock above them and began to climb down.

'But you're afraid of change. . .is that it?' Paul asked softly, and, when she didn't answer, he added, 'I think you've just got to prepare yourself for changes, Fiona, because they're going to happen.'

For a brief moment before Dominic joined them she allowed her eyes to meet his, and the expression in his made her pulses race.

At that moment Dominic jumped from the rock, landing on the grass beside them, then, losing his balance, he sat down with a bump. In an instant he was on his feet again, rubbing his bottom. 'Shall we fly the kite again now?' he asked Paul eagerly.

Paul groaned. 'Give me a minute, will you? I just want to talk to your mum for a while, then we'll start the flight of the dragon again.'

Dominic laughed and ran off again to explore the rocks, leaving the two of them watching him. As he disappeared from view Fiona felt Paul's arm around her waist, and for a brief moment she allowed herself the luxury of leaning against him. There was something in her action that seemed to symbolise her intentions, almost as if she was saying that she needed someone to lean on sometimes.

They were silent for a while, Fiona perfectly content to rest against Paul, while he gently stroked her arm, then turning her face slightly, she said, 'How well do you know Charles?'

He chuckled. 'Why, are you worrying about his

suitability for Lilli?' Then, more seriously, he added, 'I don't really know him that well, but he and my father were at university together and have kept in touch ever since. But from what I've seen of him since I've been here I'd say he's great, and so right for Lilli.' He fell silent again, then after a moment he added, 'But wasn't it a coincidence that he happened to be here and that he'd met Lilli?'

There it was again; that word coincidence, the word that for some reason kept flitting in and out of Fiona's brain, then once again she was forced to dismiss it as Paul got to his feet and reached out his hand to pull her up. Together they walked across the Common to join Dominic, with Paul keeping her hand firmly in his. If Dominic noticed he made no mention of the fact, almost as if he found it quite acceptable that his mother and his judo teacher should be so friendly.

The day turned out to be quite perfect, an oasis in a desert of uncertainty, and when finally they returned to the Close to put a tired and happy little boy to bed it was Paul who read to him about his favourite Tank Engine.

Lilli had already said she was quite happy to babysit and that Charles was coming over to help pack her pictures for the exhibition, which was now only a week away. When Fiona went upstairs to get ready for her dinner with Paul she left him and Lilli talking easily together just as they had in the old days.

She chose to wear culottes in a turquoise and

black printed pattern and a black top in a soft silky material. She had bought the culottes in a moment of mad impulse which she'd later regretted when she had doubted that she would ever have occasion to wear them. Now they seemed perfect for the evening that lay ahead. She had no idea where Paul proposed to take her, but she knew that wherever they went for dinner they would end the evening at his flat. The signals had been there all day; the look in his eyes, the touch of his hand and the pressure of his thigh against hers as they had walked together, until in the end her need and her longing had been as great as his.

She knew that her hair in its fashionable jaw-length bob was her crowning glory, and she completed the effect with a tiny ceramic slide of Oriental design. She applied a little more make-up than she usually wore, accentuating her already high cheekbones with a delicate blusher and her green eyes with smoky shadow. Then as she critically surveyed her image in the mirror she added touches of her favourite perfume to her wrists, her earlobes and between her breasts.

When she went downstairs she found Lilli alone, as Paul had gone back to his place to change. Lilli smiled at her, for she couldn't fail to notice how happy she looked.

'Do you think I could dare to hope that things are going to work out for the best?' she asked.

Fiona gave a slight shrug. 'Who can say?' she replied casually, but the light in her green eyes belied her nonchalant manner.

'He cares about you, Fe, and about Dominic, and really, you know, that's all that matters.'

'I know. . .' A frown creased her smooth forehead, and Lilli threw her a sharp glance.

'So what is it?' she questioned. 'There's still something bothering you, isn't there?'

Fiona sighed and nodded, then, walking to the window, began fiddling with the cord-pulls on the curtains. 'I don't know,' she said helplessly at last. 'I just don't know, Lilli, and that's the truth. There's something niggling at the back of my mind, and I just can't put my finger on it.'

'Maybe if you have time to talk this evening you'll be able to sort things out,' said Lilli. 'After all, you've had so little time alone. But Fe, do be careful; don't let something trivial ruin your chance of happiness.'

As Lilli was talking Fiona saw Paul's car draw up outside, and as he stepped out on to the pavement her breath caught in her throat. He looked so handsome in his silk shirt and dark suit, a perfect foil for his hair, which gleamed like spun gold. And seconds later the look in his eyes told her all she needed to know about the effect her own appearance had on him.

He took her to a quietly sophisticated French restaurant on the far side of town, and as they sat together in the elegant bar sipping aperitifs she gradually felt herself relax.

They were shown to an intimate table for two in a quiet alcove, and she knew that Paul had put a great deal of thought into the evening's arrangements. The food was exquisite, the wines excellent and the music soft, French and very romantic.

As they lingered over their coffee Paul suddenly stretched out his hand and covered hers. 'Happy?' he murmured, and a smile touched her lips as she recalled the last occasion when he had asked the same question.

She nodded in reply, then looked up as he said suddenly, 'I don't want to spoil the evening, but there's something I have to tell you.'

She found herself holding her breath as she waited for him to continue. She'd been down that road before while she had waited for Paul to tell her something, and when he had, he'd blown her world apart. At his next words, however, she felt herself relax and her foolish fears slip away as he simply explained that he had to attend a course in Bristol and would be away for the next week.

'You don't seem very upset.' He said it almost accusingly as he looked curiously at her smiling face. 'I thought you'd be devastated at the thought of not seeing me for a week.'

She laughed at his injured expression. 'Oh, I am, I am, Paul—believe me. It was just that I wondered what you were going to say, that's all.'

He was silent for a moment, tracing patterns on the heavy cream tablecloth with the blunt edge of a knife. 'You still can't allow yourself to trust me completely, can you?' he asked softly.

Fiona flushed, avoiding his gaze, and he sighed.

'Well, I can't say I blame you under the circumstances. But I want you to trust me. You can, you know, Fe. I love you,' he leaned forward and his tone grew faintly husky, 'and I think by now you know what I want. I won't hurt you again. . . I swear it. Do you believe me?'

She hesitated and his grip tightened on her hand. 'Are you prepared to take the risk with me again and give me another chance?'

Still she hesitated, and he frowned. 'Do you love me, Fe?'

At last she allowed her gaze to meet his. 'Yes, Paul,' she replied softly, 'I do love you. I always have. My feelings have never changed.'

He flinched at the implication. 'I know. . .it was me who loused things up the first time, but at least I've tried to put things right now.'

She frowned. 'But it was only chance that we met again. . .a coincidence. . .' She trailed off abruptly, troubled by the word coincidence again.

Paul remained silent, his eyes downcast, and there was something in his silence that bothered her. 'Paul,' she said at last as something incomprehensible began stirring in the recesses of her mind. He glanced up, but she was unable to interpret the expression on his face. 'Paul. . .it was only by chance that we met again, wasn't it?'

'What do you mean?' This time it was him avoiding her gaze.

'Well, it's just that there seem to have been so many coincidences. . .too many, in fact,' she added. 'For a start, the fact that we end up working not only in the same hospital but on the same unit. Then the fact that Charles Farnsworth just happens to be an old friend of your father's and then, probably most incredible of all, you end up taking judo lessons and teaching a little boy who turns out to be your own son.' She was aware that her voice had started to rise.

Paul, in an obvious attempt to ease the tension, gave a light laugh. 'Well, they do say fact is stranger than fiction, but it was no coincidence that Dominic and I got on so well. We hit it off right from the start.'

Fiona stared at him, noting the pride in his eyes as he spoke of Dominic, and it was then that a sudden flash of intuition finally struck her and the things that had been bothering her began to form some sort of order in her mind. 'You knew he was your son, didn't you, Paul?' she said slowly. 'You knew before you started teaching him judo?'

'Yes, Fiona, I knew,' he replied quietly.

'When did you know?' Her tone had changed, and he must have noticed, because he threw her an anxious glance, then as he took a deep breath she abruptly withdrew her hand from beneath his.

'It's a long story, and I was going to tell you——'

'When?'

He glanced up and frowned.

'When were you going to tell me?'

'When I considered it to be the right time. . .'

'How long have you known?' Her voice was dull

now, devoid of all emotion, and Paul began to look anxious.

'I knew last year, Fiona.'

'Last year? But you've only been here a few weeks!' He was silent as she glared angrily at him across the table. 'Who told you, Paul? Who told you about Dominic?'

'Edward Partridge.'

'Who?' She continued to stare at him, then she shook her head slightly as the name rang a bell in her mind. 'Partridge? You mean the registrar at Birmingham?'

He nodded. 'Yes, except that he's a surgeon now.'

'I don't care what he is! He should learn to mind his own business. I suppose he told you we'd moved to Merstonbury as well?'

'Yes, he did, as a matter of fact——'

'So you thought you'd come here and unbeknown to me get to know my son?'

'No, Fiona, it wasn't like that——'

'You know, Paul, you'd take first prize for deviousness.'

'Fiona! Will you please let me explain?'

'Explain what? I suppose you're now going to say that Charles Farnsworth wasn't a coincidence either, that he was in on it as well—did he get you the job here? And what about Lilli? Did you recruit her as well?' Fiona was furious now, her voice filled with bitterness as the full implication of what Paul had done finally hit her. She hardly heard him as he patiently tried to explain that the presence of Charles Farnsworth in Merstonbury had indeed been a coincidence.

'Well, it was the only thing that was,' she retorted at last. 'As far as I can see, everything else was contrived, and for the past month while you've been so busy chatting me up—you knew everything. Why didn't you tell me?' she ended furiously.

'I was afraid of your reaction—and it looks as if I had just cause,' Paul added drily. When she didn't immediately reply he said, 'I felt I had to tread very carefully—you'd brought Dominic up virtually alone and I thought you might resent any intrusion from me.'

'You're too right I would!' she blazed. 'I had doubts from the start about trusting you again, and it looks as if I was right!'

'I'm sorry, Fiona, I thought it was better this way.'

'What way? Spying on me? Lying? Using every devious trick in the book to get Dominic to like you? And, if that wasn't enough, making me look a fool into the bargain!'

'I don't understand, how have I made you look a fool?'

'By not telling me—by leading me to believe it was me you wanted, when all along it was only the fact that you had a son that intrigued you!'

'Fiona, listen to me—you've got it all wrong. It *is* you I want. Dominic is a wonderful bonus, but it's you I want.'

'Then why didn't you tell me? Don't you think I had a right to know?'

There was a heavy silence as she continued to glare at him, then he sighed and, very quietly, he said, 'If it's rights we're talking about, then don't you think that for the past six years I had the right to know I had a son?' There was a sudden steely glint in his eyes, making them appear bleak without their usual hint of amusement.

Fiona stood up, pushing her chair back with a sudden screech that made everyone else in the restaurant look up with startled interest. Then with a final angry gesture she flung down her napkin. 'Maybe, Paul. Maybe not,' she said through gritted teeth. 'But if you've come back here with any intention of taking him from me then you can forget it. I doubt there's a court in the country that would give you custody!'

With her cheeks burning she strode from the restaurant past the other diners and into the street, leaving Paul to settle the bill.

CHAPTER ELEVEN

OUTSIDE Fiona glanced up and down the High Street, then, seeing a taxi rank on the opposite side, she hurried across and hired one of the cabs to take her back to the Close. She took her seat just in time to see Paul as he came out of the restaurant and stood on the kerb. As the taxi pulled away she knew he had seen her, but she kept her eyes ahead, giving no indication that she had seen him. There was a strange sick feeling deep in the pit of her stomach, and it had nothing to do with the meal she had just eaten.

At the Close Lilli was fortunately too involved with assisting Charles with the packing of her pictures to notice that Fiona was home much earlier than she would have been if her evening had gone as planned. Consequently Fiona was able to escape to her room without any awkward questions being asked, and it wasn't until she was in bed that she finally gave vent to her anger and heartbreak in a storm of weeping. If only she hadn't given in to her feelings! If only she'd taken heed of her own intuition, which had continually warned her against making the same mistakes again. If only she hadn't allowed herself to be sweet-talked by Paul into trusting him again. For a moment there she had almost believed him, had

160

almost dared to hope that they might have a future together, only to find that all along he had lied to her.

Her anger was still simmering under the surface the following morning when she arrived at work. She was only thankful that Paul had gone to Bristol on his course and at least she wouldn't have to face him for the time being. She did, however, have to face Jill, who took one look at her and immediately knew something was very wrong.

Gently her friend took her by the arm. 'What is it, Fiona?' she asked. 'Can I help?'

Fiona shook her head, biting her lip furiously to quell the sudden rush of tears that threatened at the sudden words of concern. 'No,' she muttered. 'I'm all right, really.'

'Well, you don't look all right.' Jill stared keenly at her. 'Fiona, is it Paul Sheldon?' she asked quietly, so that the rest of the staff wouldn't hear.

Fiona looked up, startled, then, lowering her eyes again, she nodded. She suddenly had an overwhelming desire to confide in her friend.

'Listen, we can't talk now,' said Jill as other staff began arriving and the night staff prepared to leave. 'But have lunch with me later; we'll buy some sandwiches and take them outside where we won't be disturbed.'

Fiona nodded, then made a superhuman attempt to blot the previous evening from her mind and concentrate on the job in hand.

It was to be a big day for Jim Evans, who was going to get out of bed for the first time after his period of total bed-rest. Stuart McVey arrived, and, assisted by Fiona, carefully rolled Mr Evans to the edge of his bed, strapped him into a surgical corset to support his spine, then very slowly eased him to his feet.

'How are you feeling, Jim?' Fiona smiled at Mr Evans, who was clutching at the two of them for support and looking very pale.

'I feel drained right out,' he replied. 'As if someone just pulled a plug on me!'

Stuart laughed. 'That's the first time I've heard anyone describe it like that,' he said, then, glancing at Fiona, he added, 'Right, Staff, I think that's enough to start with. Let's get him back to bed.'

'Oh, I thought you were going to make me run round the block,' sighed Jim Evans, as he sank thankfully back on to his bed.

'No, that'll be later today,' said Fiona as she unbuckled his corset.

Jim gave a weak laugh.

'You think she's joking, don't you?' Stuart chuckled. 'But you see, we'll be back after lunch. We won't give you a minute's rest now. Staff here will have you up making beds tomorrow morning.' He moved away to see David Amery, whose bed Fiona had moved next to Simon's.

Fiona straightened Jim Evans's covers and handed him his personal stereo, which had helped him through his tedious period of bed rest. 'Are you feeling all right, Jim?' she asked.

'I'll be OK in a minute. I just feel dizzy.'

'That's understandable after being so long on

your back. You'll have to take things very slowly to start with, gradually increasing what you do each day,' she said, then, glancing up, she added, 'Ah, here comes your coffee. I expect you'll feel you've earned that this morning.'

While the patients were drinking their morning coffee the consultants arrived for their round. Fiona was caught unawares, and as they suddenly appeared her heart jumped, then she remembered that Paul wasn't with them and she relaxed a little.

She was kept very busy until lunchtime with further admissions, one of whom was a woman of forty with secondary bone cancer. Fiona knew she would require much careful nursing as the prognosis was not good and she was as yet unaware that she only had a short while to live.

It seemed no time at all before Jill appeared in the office and asked if she was ready for lunch. They left the building and strolled in the grounds, enjoying the fact that the wind had at last dropped, giving way to a soft warm April day. They headed for a seat positioned against a backdrop of blazing forsythia and, sitting down, automatically raised their faces to the sun.

After they had given themselves time to unwind from the pressures of the grim realities of the ward, they unpacked the sandwiches they'd bought from the canteen. It was Jill who finally broached the question that hung in the air between them.

'So are you going to tell me all about it, then?'

she said, casually biting deep into her corned beef sandwich.

Fiona sighed and fiddled with the clingfilm that covered her lunch. During the morning she had decided that she wouldn't give away too much to Jill, but her friend's next words took her completely unawares.

'Paul is Dominic's father, isn't he?' she asked quietly, without looking up.

Fiona threw her a startled glance, a denial springing to her lips, then she sighed and, leaning her head back, closed her eyes briefly. Then at last she spoke. 'How did you know?'

'It wasn't too difficult. There is just a bit of resemblance there, you know. Come on, Fiona, even Barry saw it, and usually he can never see likenesses.'

Jill fell silent, obviously waiting for her to continue, and suddenly, her lunch forgotten on her lap, Fiona started to speak, and before she knew where she was she was telling Jill the whole story.

Her friend listened attentively without interruption, and when Fiona finally finished with details of the row in the restaurant the previous evening she remained silent.

'So what do you think?' Fiona demanded at last.

'I think you over-reacted,' Jill replied firmly.

'What?' Fiona stared at her in astonishment. She had been sure that Jill would see things from her side.

'I don't think you gave him enough chance to explain.'

'What was there to explain, for heaven's sake?'

Jill stirred restlessly on the wooden seat. 'Let's try and think about this rationally,' she said, and, when Fiona remained stubbornly silent, she went on, 'What do you think happened? What I mean is, how did you really think you and Paul met again after all that time?'

'I imagined it was purely by chance, just one of those things.'

'And what did you think happened then?'

'That, after seeing me again, he wanted to resume our relationship.'

'And how did you feel about that?'

'At first I was dubious; he'd already left me once and I wondered what his reaction would be when he found out about Dominic. But when he did, he still seemed to want to continue, but now. . .now I know it didn't happen like that at all, it changes everything.'

'So what actually happened? Tell me again, slowly this time,' said Jill.

'Well, some time last year there was a chance meeting, but it was between Paul and a man called Edward Partridge, someone we both knew in the old days. Apparently he told Paul that I'd had a child and later moved to Merstonbury. It was only then, when Paul found out he had a son, that he decided to track me down. From that moment the whole thing was contrived; his job here, his trying to date me again and even the devious way he got to know Dominic behind my back. Honestly, Jill,

I'm so angry with him! Why couldn't he have told me?'

'I'm sorry, Fiona, but I can't see what all the fuss is about. What does it matter how he found out? He's here now and he knows, and he still seems to want you, and Dominic. I really think you're making a mountain out of a molehill.' Jill glanced sympathetically at her friend, and, seeing her miserable look, she reached out her hand and briefly touched her arm.

'But how do I know I can trust him again?' Fiona asked, and there was real anguish in her tone.

Jill shrugged. 'You don't, but that goes for any of us. Human nature being what it is, we can never be completely certain of anyone, and that includes ourselves. What you need to do is think about what you might be throwing away, for yourself and for Dominic.'

Jill's words had practically echoed Lilli's feelings, and as Fiona returned to the ward after her lunch break she found herself questioning her reactions to what had happened. Had she over-reacted? Had she been unfair to Paul, and was she really throwing away her chance of happiness? Suddenly she felt exhausted by the whole thing, and she began to think it was a good job that Paul had gone away for a week. At least it gave them both a breathing-space, time to examine their feelings and establish what they really wanted.

When she walked on to the ward she found that David Amery had the phone trolley by his bed and was deep in conversation with someone. Simon was watching his portable television which he'd persuaded the staff to fix up at the foot of his bed and the rest of the ward seemed relatively quiet. Fiona found Kelly and Betty Stevens checking supplies in the store, and Betty told her that Stuart McVey was on his way to the ward to help with Jim Evans again.

Fiona glanced at her watch, 'I'd like to get that over and Jim back to bed before any visitors arrive,' she remarked.

Betty nodded. 'Yes, it can get a bit hectic.' She grinned at Kelly. 'Like yesterday, eh, Kelly?'

The young student blushed. 'Yes, it did get a bit out of hand, didn't it?'

'Why, what happened?' Fiona looked mystified.

'It was Simon's visitors,' explained Kelly. 'Honestly, that boy'll be the death of me! I heard all this commotion, and when I went in he had no less than nine of them round his bed, all friends that he was at school with. I tried to get rid of them, you know, telling them only two to a bed, but Simon turns on the charm, like he does, and I don't get anywhere. I just start to panic because of the noise—although I must say the other patients seemed to be enjoying it—when Sister Buchanan suddenly appears like a galleon in full sail. She stands at the top of the ward and doesn't say a word. She just looks! And do you know what? They went. . .just like that. Honestly, Staff, I nearly died!'

As Kelly finished relating her story the physiotherapist arrived, and as Fiona accompanied him to Jim Evans's bed she found herself chuckling over what had happened the day before.

It proved to be quite an event in the ward when Jim Evans finally took his first steps after being flat on his back for three weeks. With the help of Stuart McVey and a walking-frame and encouragement from Fiona and his fellow patients, he walked carefully down the centre of the ward. At the end he rested a while against the back of a chair, then slowly made his way back to his bed.

'You've done very well, Jim,' said Fiona as she helped him into bed. 'If all goes well I should think we'd be able to let you go home at the end of the week.'

At her words Jim's face lit up. 'Do you really think so, Nurse?'

'As long as you don't go overdoing things. It'll be a long time before you're feeling really fit, you know.'

Once Fiona had Jim settled she had a word with Simon and David, who were engrossed in a quiz game, then she prepared to go off duty as her shift was over for the day.

It was as she was leaving the hospital by the main entrance that Fiona almost collided with a young girl. She murmured an apology, then stopped and looked back as she recognised the girl. She too had stopped, and when she realised it was Fiona she laughingly hurried back to her.

'Hello, Nurse,' she said.

'Hello, Tracy,' Fiona replied, then raised her eyebrows.

'He phoned me!' explained the girl excitedly, pushing back her long hair. 'He phoned about an hour ago. He said he wanted to see me and that he was missing me.'

'Oh, Tracy, I'm so pleased,' replied Fiona happily.

'I'd like to thank you, Nurse. I'm sure you had something to do with this.'

Fiona shrugged. 'Not really. All I did was to move his bed.'

Tracy frowned. 'I don't understand.'

'You'll see,' Fiona replied. 'I think it was simply a question of David's finding out that there are others worse off than himself who've learned to come to terms with their disabilities and who are living life to the full.'

Tracy looked mystified, and Fiona smiled. 'You go in and you'll see what I mean,' she said, then, leaving Tracy to go and find David, she set off for home.

It proved to be a strange week for Fiona, because, although at the beginning she was relieved that Paul had gone away, by Wednesday evening she found she was missing him dreadfully. This feeling was intensified when she went to read Dominic his bedtime story.

She was halfway through one of his favourite stories by Roald Dahl when she realised he wasn't listening.

'What's wrong, Dominic?' she asked as she lowered the book and stared at him.

He stirred restlessly on his pillow. 'I was just thinking about Paul,' he told her.

'What were you thinking?' she asked casually, but only too aware that her heart was hammering at the mere mention of Paul's name.

'I was wondering when he's going to come and see us again.'

'Well, he's away at the moment,' she said carefully. 'He's gone to Bristol on a course.'

'What's a course?' Dominic gazed at her solemnly.

'Well. . .' she hesitated, 'it's like lessons. . .learning something new.'

'Like school?' He stared at her unbelievingly, as if he found it impossible that Paul could be actually going to school.

Fiona nodded. 'Yes, something like that. There's always something to learn, you know. Do you like Paul, Dominic?' she added, and found herself holding her breath as she waited for his reply. Since her talk with Jill she had found that her attitude had changed slightly towards Paul and what he had done. Jill had made her see things in a vastly different light.

'Yes, he's great,' her son replied enthusiastically. 'He's the best kite-flier I know. You're pretty good, Mum,' he added generously, 'for a girl. But Paul is ace!'

Most of her spare time for the rest of the week was taken up with helping Lilli with her exhibition, which was to open with a small reception at the gallery on Saturday lunchtime. The guests were to be mainly friends and people of Lilli's acquaintance from the art world. Charles Farnsworth had put a great deal of help and effort into the preparations, and it was his car that was at their disposal to ferry the pictures from the Close to the gallery. Lilli herself supervised the actual hanging of the paintings with the help of Fiona and the gallery staff, and by late on Friday evening they were all in place.

As Lilli stood back critically surveying her work, Fiona slipped her arm through hers. 'They're wonderful, you know,' she said softly. 'Quite the best you've ever done.'

'Oh, darling, do you really think so?' Lilli gave a tired smile, and Fiona knew that this exhibition had taken its toll and that her mother was exhausted.

'Yes, I do. You've caught the light in your landscapes in a way you've never done before— almost as if you've been inspired by something— or someone.' She smiled as her gaze flicked towards Charles, who was clearing away the last of the packing materials.

'Maybe I have,' replied Lilli softly, allowing her own gaze to follow Fiona's. 'He's been wonderful, you know, Fe, and he's so concerned about me working too hard. Do you know, he even wants to take me to Madeira for a holiday after the exhibition.'

'But that's wonderful!' exclaimed Fiona, then, catching sight of her mother's face, she said, 'You will go?'

Lilli hesitated. 'Well, I told him we'd have to see, because of Dominic. . .'

'I'll worry about Dominic,' said Fiona firmly.

'But your job, darling. . .'

'Don't you worry, we'll sort something out,' said Fiona.

Lilli smiled. 'Can I take that to mean that things may be happening for you as well?' she asked.

'Who knows?' Fiona replied brightly. 'We'll just have to wait and see.' She hadn't told Lilli about her argument with Paul and she had no intention of worrying her at the present time. She was saved from any further questioning as Charles crossed the gallery to join them with a welcome suggestion of a drink in the wine-bar next door.

Later that night, after she had paid the baby-sitter she'd employed for the evening and was sitting in front of her mirror preparing for bed, she found herself thinking about her conversation with Lilli. It really wasn't fair that Lilli was unable to live her own life because of the responsibility of Dominic. Fiona knew she would be eternally grateful to her mother for all the help she'd given her in the past, but the time had come now to release her from those commitments. But just how she was going to achieve this Fiona had no idea.

Helplessly she gazed at her reflection. If only things had worked out differently between herself and Paul! She had wondered if he would phone her during the week he was in Bristol, but he hadn't, and she now took that to mean that the things she had said to him at the restaurant had made him realise there was no point in pursuing the matter. It was her own fault—Jill had made her see that—but at the time she had been so angry with him, and she had honestly believed that she could have no future with a man she believed had lied to her.

So why was it that now she was missing him so much? Why was it that she was bitterly regretting her outburst? With a sigh she turned away from the mirror. Deep down she knew the answers to her own questions, just as she knew that she had never in all the years since she had met Paul stopped loving him. And now, through her own stupidity, it looked as if she had thrown away her chance of happiness.

CHAPTER TWELVE

THEY were up and dressed early the following morning, and when Charles arrived immediately after breakfast it was agreed that he would take Lilli down to the gallery while Fiona would collect Neil and take the boys to their judo lesson.

'I'll meet you at the gallery as soon as I can,' said Fiona. 'The caterers should be there by then, so I'll be able to lend a hand with the food.' She glanced anxiously at her mother as she spoke. Lilli seemed even more vague than usual that morning. 'Are you all right?' she asked gently.

Lilli nodded and sighed. 'Yes, I think so.'

'Are you nervous?' Fiona was curious, for she'd never known Lilli to be nervous about her work in the past.

'I suppose I must be. Somehow I don't quite seem to have the confidence I had when I was younger, and this is the biggest show I've ever done.'

'But aren't you forgetting something?' Fiona asked softly, as Dominic suddenly hurtled down the stairs and landed in a heap at their feet.

Lilli raised her eyebrows enquiringly.

'Not only is it your biggest show, it also happens to be your best.'

Lilli's eyes had been clouded with anxiety, but

at Fiona's words they visibly brightened. 'You really think so?' she whispered.

'I know so,' Fiona replied firmly, then, catching Dominic's hand, she said, 'Right, come on, monster, let's get going!'

Lilli, looking much happier, saw them off with a wave and a smile, while Dominic, with his shoulders hunched, lurched down the path, giving his best monster impression.

There was a slight chill in the air from the mist that hung over the city, obscuring the top of the Cathedral, but the April sun was hovering, searching for a way through and promising a warm bright day. They walked the short distance to Neil's house, where Jane had him ready and waiting for his judo lesson.

'I'll pick the boys up afterwards,' said Jane. 'Then I'll bring Dominic down to the gallery.'

'Thanks, Jane, that's kind of you. I want to be there to give Lilli all the support I can today,' said Fiona, adding, 'But why don't you and Neil come in and have a drink and a sausage roll? Lilli said we could ask any friends we like.'

'That's very nice of you,' replied Jane as she walked to the gate with them, 'but my parents are coming over for the day, so we'll have to get back.'

As they walked to the leisure centre the boys began discussing who would be most likely to give them their lesson that morning.

'I bet it'll be Stinky Saunders,' said Dominic, pulling a face.

'No, I reckon it'll be Mr Sheldon,' replied Neil hopefully.

'No, it won't, he's on a. . . on a course, isn't he, Mum?' Dominic looked up at Fiona and, when she nodded, he went on, 'And it's Dr Sheldon, not Mr, but he said that I could call him Paul, because he's a friend of my mum, isn't he, Mum?' He looked up again, and when she nodded for the second time he glanced at Neil to make sure he was suitably impressed.

Fiona, in fact, was feeling uncertain, because she had no idea when Paul was returning from Bristol, and as they drew nearer to the leisure centre her heart began to pound uncomfortably.

But there was no sign of his silver-coloured Rover in the car park, and it was with a sigh of relief that she left the boys in the changing-rooms. She just didn't feel she could cope with meeting Paul at that precise moment. She had enough on her plate for one day coping with Lilli.

The gallery was an elegant suite of rooms on the first floor of an old house in the High Street. The ground floor housed the offices of a building society, while the top floor was converted into flats.

Fiona arrived just as the caterers' vans pulled up and two men from the local radio station began carrying equipment from a Land Rover into the building and up the wide staircase. She was grateful to find that Charles Farnsworth seemed to have everything under control, while Lilli's friend from the nearby florist's shop had decorated the reception area with several pedestals of spring flowers.

When all the preparations were complete Fiona managed to find a small cloakroom to change into the outfit that Jane had made for her especially for the occasion. It was a full-skirted dress of soft silky material in a shade of green that matched her eyes. She had carefully teamed it with a pair of deep purple shoes and beads and earrings of the same colour. The overall effect against her crown of blonde hair was startling, and Fiona felt well pleased as she made her way to Lilli's side to help her greet the guests who were beginning to arrive.

Lilli herself flitted around like a beautiful butterfly in an exquisite creation of layers of chiffon in delicate pastel shades of lilac, mauve and blue. Fiona was pleased to see that she looked happy and serene, with no sign of her earlier nerves. At one point she caught her laughing up into Charles's face, and she felt a momentary pang as she saw the return message in his eyes. If only, she thought, things could have been different between herself and Paul—but there was now little doubt in her mind that she had ruined everything. It certainly didn't look as if there was anything in Merstonbury to induce him to hurry back from Bristol.

Within half an hour Fiona could see that the exhibition was going well and that Lilli's paintings were being acclaimed, while Lilli herself had relaxed, and with a glass of champagne in one hand was chatting in an animated fashion to a group of dealers.

It was some time later as she was talking to the art critic from the local *Recorder* that Fiona happened to glance up and catch sight of Dominic. Murmuring an apology to the reporter, she made her way through the crowd of people across the vast room.

Dominic seemed to be talking to someone who was hidden from Fiona's view by an ornamental pillar, and she thought perhaps Jane and Neil had come in after all. As she approached, however, Dominic turned and saw her.

'Hi, Mum,' he said, and grinned up at her. 'Neil couldn't come, and you did say I could bring a friend, didn't you?'

'Well, yes. . .' She trailed off, then her eyes widened as Paul stepped from behind the pillar. Her heart leapt as their eyes met. 'Why, Paul, what are you doing here? I thought you were in Bristol,' she said.

'I was,' he answered. 'But I had to get back in time for a certain judo lesson.' He smiled down at Dominic, then looked back at Fiona, and suddenly it was as if their quarrel had never been. All she wanted was to walk into his arms and have him hold her tight.

Whether or not he felt the same she didn't know, but there was a look in his eyes that she recognised, a look which threatened that at any moment he just might disregard the sixty or so people who thronged the gallery. Hastily she spoke, to try to avert what could easily turn out to be an embarrassing episode. 'How was your course?' she asked, and was amazed that her voice could sound so normal when her stomach was churning and her knees were knocking so loudly that surely everyone must hear.

The familiar look of amusement was in his eyes. 'Much like any other course,' he replied.

'But did you learn anything?' asked Dominic solemnly.

'Dominic!' gasped Fiona, while Paul chuckled.

'I hope I did,' he replied, raising his eyebrows at Fiona.

To cover her embarrassment, she said, 'Dominic wanted to know where you were, and, when I told him, he wanted to know what a course was.'

Paul glanced down at his son. 'Did you miss me, old chap?' he asked, and there was no denying the pleasure in his voice.

Dominic nodded without hesitation. 'Yes, I wanted to fly the kite again, but Mum's been busy.'

'I dare say she has this week,' Paul replied, and glanced round the gallery as he spoke. 'But maybe, if Mum agrees, we can go again tomorrow.'

'Can we?' demanded Dominic, pulling at Fiona's arm.

'I expect so,' she replied weakly. Things seemed to be moving much faster than she had intended, and as she caught Paul's eye she realised that he had read her thoughts.

'We need to talk before then, don't we?' he murmured so that only she heard.

She nodded. 'Yes, Paul, we do.'

'Will Lilli be at home tonight?'

'No, Charles is taking her out to celebrate.'

He smiled. 'Quite right too. She deserves it after all her hard work. All right if I come over later?'

'Yes, come and have supper with Dominic and me. He's been saving the rest of the Tank Engine story for you to read. Now, I must go and circulate.' As she moved away, leaving Dominic quite happy with the friend he had chosen to bring, Fiona was aware of a warm glow which had started somewhere deep inside and was rapidly spreading throughout her entire body.

It was quite dark by the time they had eaten supper, and Dominic, worn out by the excitement of the day, had listened to only half his story before falling into a sound sleep. Paul crept from his bedroom and joined Fiona in the kitchen, where he helped her to wash the dishes. The coffee bubbled in the percolator and its delicious aroma filled the tiny house.

As she reached up to a cupboard for cups and saucers, she suddenly felt Paul's arms go around her, and as she leaned against him he buried his face in her neck, gently biting her earlobe.

After a while he lifted his head and murmured, 'Do you know something? At this precise moment I have everything I want within these four walls; the woman I love, my child sleeping upstairs and a taste of domestic bliss. I never thought I'd hear myself say it, but it's true—can you believe me, Fiona?'

She turned her head and, raising her hand, she gently ran her fingers down the side of his face. 'I owe you an apology, Paul, for running out on you last week, and another for doubting you.'

He shook his head. 'I got exactly what I asked for—I should have told you earlier.' Turning her to face him, he slipped his arms around her waist, holding her close as his mouth found hers in a kiss that confirmed what he had just said. A kiss so full of passion and desire that it kindled a similar longing deep inside herself.

A long time later he drew away. 'Will you give me a chance to explain?' he asked softly, and, when she nodded, he picked up the tray with the coffee and, following her into the living-room, set the tray down on a low table, then sat closely beside her on the sofa.

'So what is there to explain?' she asked, turning her head to study his profile.

'A great deal,' he answered.

She frowned. 'I don't understand. . .you've already told me about meeting Edward Partridge. . .'

'I know, but you gave me no chance to say how I met him.'

'How you met him? I imagined you just bumped into one another by chance.'

'I know that's what you thought.' Paul smiled and, leaning forward, poured the coffee, handing her a cup. 'But it wasn't quite like that. You see, I deliberately went back to Birmingham.'

'But why?' She stared at him.

'To find you.' His reply was simple, but its effect was to stir a thread of hope deep inside her. He sighed and, setting his cup and saucer down on the table, he took a deep breath. 'Do you remember, Fiona, my telling you how I often thought about you? Well, the truth was I couldn't get you out of my mind. Oh, I know it was a long time and obviously there were periods when I just got on with my life, but every so often, usually when I was least expecting it, you'd flit back into my mind. In the end I couldn't stand it any longer, and I knew I had to find out what had happened to you.' He was silent for a moment, as if marshalling his thoughts, then, glancing at her again, he continued with his story.

'The obvious place to start seemed to be Shrewsbury, so I went there first. But it was as if you'd vanished off the face of the earth. The house where Lilli had lived had changed hands twice, and the present occupiers didn't have any idea where she had gone. From there it seemed logical to go to the hospital in Birmingham, which is where I found old Partridge.'

'I never did like that man,' said Fiona. 'I suppose he took great delight in telling you I had to leave to have a baby.'

Paul paused long enough for her to look up enquiringly, then slowly he said, 'Actually, it was quite the reverse.'

'What do you mean?' she asked suspiciously.

'Well, he seemed to assume that we must be married and living happily in Merstonbury. He even asked if we'd had any more children.'

'What?' Fiona set her cup down on the table with a clatter and stared at him incredulously. 'Why should he have thought that?'

Paul shrugged. 'Well, he never did have the best memory in the world, and I suppose events got a bit muddled in his mind. He knew you and I had been going together for some time, that we left around the same time, and somehow he knew that you were expecting a baby. No doubt some well-meaning soul told him that you'd moved to Merstonbury and he just jumped to the wrong conclusions.'

She was silent as she tried to digest what Paul had just told her, but somewhere at the back of her mind a small voice was telling her over and over that he had gone back for her before he'd known that she'd had his child. 'But what did you think? How did you feel after he'd told you all that?' she asked at last, hardly daring to look at his face.

'I was devastated. I just didn't know what to think. The next day I took the train here to Merstonbury and checked into the Rose and Crown for a few days.'

'Did you see me during that time?' she asked sharply.

He nodded. 'Yes, I saw you several times.'

'But why didn't you make yourself known? I

don't understand. . .why. . .?' Her voice began to rise, and, turning towards her, he took her hands in his.

'Fiona, please, don't get upset again. Please listen and try to understand why I acted as I did. I know it must seem as if I was spying on you, but, please believe me, it wasn't like that.'

She shook her head, but before she could voice any further protest he went on hurriedly, 'You must try and see it from my point of view. You see, I realised very quickly that your son was mine as well, but I didn't know how you'd react to my sudden appearance in your life again.'

'I know, but——'

'No, hear me out. . .please?' As she fell silent again he continued, 'I had to come to terms with the fact that for some reason of your own you had chosen not to inform me that I had a son. You'd then apparently gone on to bring him up quite successfully on your own. Another aspect for me to consider was whether or not there was any other man in your life. Anyway, while I was in Merstonbury I met up with Peter Simpson, who told me about the registrar's job that was coming up at St Catherine's. I went back to London, but I thought about it long and hard and eventually, when the job became vacant, I decided to apply. When I heard that I'd got it I almost chickened out. I hadn't seriously thought I stood a chance.

'I moved to Merstonbury and managed to rent the place down by the canal from a friend, and, suddenly, there I was and there you were, cool and efficient, running the orthopaedic unit and looking even more beautiful than before. From that first day when we met in the office I knew I hadn't made a mistake in coming back.' As Paul was speaking his grip tightened on her hands while his eyes never left hers. 'You see, Fiona, I'd never stopped loving you. It took me long enough to realise it, but it's the truth. All I can do now is hope you'll believe it.'

'And what about Dominic?' she asked slowly.

'Dominic?' He frowned. 'What about him? As far as I'm concerned he's the greatest little guy that walked this earth—but I'm probably prejudiced.'

'That isn't what I meant.' She smiled in spite of herself, for she rapidly felt the situation was slipping from her control and any argument she might have put forward was evaporating. 'I was referring to the judo lessons and your making friends with Dominic behind my back.'

'Ah, now there you have me!' Paul made an attempt to look contrite. 'I must confess, that was a put-up job. I saw you taking him to the leisure centre one Saturday morning, even before I'd started work at the hospital. I made a few enquiries, and I must say I was tickled pink when I knew he was having judo lessons—I figured you couldn't hate me that much if you were encouraging our son in my favourite sport. Anyway, as luck would have it, they were looking for someone to help out with some of the lessons, and I seemed to fit the bill.'

'I expect your being a black belt might have had something to do with it,' replied Fiona drily.

Paul laughed and, releasing her hands, he slipped one arm around her shoulders, drawing her against him.

'Maybe, maybe not. But I didn't want to rush anyone, you or Dominic. I figured I'd like to get to know him before he knew who I was.'

'So what would you have done if Marilyn Hughes hadn't opened her mouth that day and told you about Dominic?'

He laughed. 'I suppose that was done to put me off you? I must admit it threw me at the time.'

'But when would you have told me that you knew?' Fiona persisted.

He shrugged. 'I don't know. I guess I was waiting for you to tell me. . .'

'And I was going through agonies wondering whether to tell you or not. Lilli thought I was mad.'

'What did she think you should do?'

'Oh, she thought I should just welcome you back with open arms and forget the past seven years.'

'Sensible lady, your mother.'

'The trouble with Lilli is that she always did have a soft spot for you,' commented Fiona, pulling a face and snuggling closer to him.

'As I said, sensible lady,' he repeated with a laugh. He was silent for a moment, as if reflecting, and at the same time he began caressing her shoulder, then he commented, 'It looks as if I was right about Lilli and Charles, doesn't it?'

'It does,' Fiona admitted, then, lifting her head so that she could watch his expression, she said, 'He's even asked her to go to Madeira with him on holiday.'

'Good for Charles! Is she going?'

'She will if I have anything to do with it,' said Fiona darkly.

Paul frowned and for a moment stopped caressing her. 'Is there a problem?'

'Nothing that can't be sorted out. She was worrying about looking after Dominic.'

He was silent again, then slowly he said, 'Fiona, Dominic is as much my concern now as yours, providing, of course, that you'll let him be.'

'What do you mean?'

'Well,' he replied, apparently choosing his words with care, 'after we're married we'll share the responsibility of caring for Dominic.'

In the silence that followed Fiona sat upright, then slowly turned to face him. 'Oh?' she asked innocently. 'Are we getting married?'

'Of course,' he replied firmly. 'You don't think I'm going to let you go again, do you?'

When she didn't answer immediately, he said, 'It is what you want as well, isn't it?'

She nodded. 'Oh, yes, more than anything else!'

'We have a lot of time to make up, and I dare say we'll have our difficulties. For a start, Dominic may not accept me.'

'I shouldn't think there's much danger of that.'

Fiona smiled. 'He already thinks you're ace, and if someone is ace—well, that's it!'

Paul chuckled. 'I can't wait to start being a proper father, but first I'd like a bit of practice at being a husband.' Leaning towards her, he kissed her lightly on the lips. 'But I don't want you worrying about anything. We'll sort something out as regards looking after Dominic,' he said, adding, 'I don't want you to put your career in jeopardy.'

She considered for a moment. 'You know something, Paul? I may just want to put my career on ice for a while and enjoy some time with Dominic.'

He stared at her, as if he couldn't believe his ears. 'I never thought I'd hear you say that, not after all your hard work to get where you have,' he said.

She shrugged lightly. 'There are some things that are more important, like attending open days at school and taking your child to the Adventure Park and not just hearing about everything second-hand. And there's another thing. . .' she paused and glanced up at him '. . . I always did worry about Dominic's being an only child.'

As the implication of what she was saying dawned on Paul, he gathered her into his arms and held her very, very close, so close that she could hear the steady beating of his heart.

'I never dared to hope that you might want more children,' he murmured, his lips against her hair, then seriously, he added, 'But what about your career? That sister's post is almost yours, and you wanted it so much.'

Fiona sighed. 'I know I did, but that was before. Things have changed now. I think I might just enjoy the idea of being a wife and mother for a while—and besides, I can always go back to my career in the future.' Suddenly she chuckled.

'What is it?' asked Paul, as he dropped gentle butterfly kisses on her forehead, her eyelids and the tip of her nose.

'I was just thinking, I know one person who would be absolutely delighted if I were to leave St Catherine's.'

'You mean Lilli?'

She shook her head. 'No, I was thinking of Marilyn Hughes. She may have lost her chance with you, Paul, but she would be the only contender for the job.' She laughed, then added, 'And yes, of course Lilli will be delighted as well.'

Gently he cupped her chin and tilted her face upwards, entangling his hands in her hair as he did so, then, just before his lips met hers again, he said, 'Talking of Lilli, did she happen to say what time they'd be home?'

Fiona lifted her face to his. 'She did; they'll be late.'

'Good,' he murmured. 'So I would say that tonight there's very little chance of our being disturbed.'

— MEDICAL ROMANCE —

The books for your enjoyment this month are:

ALWAYS ON MY MIND Laura Macdonald
TANSY'S CHILDREN Alice Grey
A BITTER JUDGEMENT Marion Lennox
HAWAIIAN HEALING Sara Burton

♥   ♥   ♥   ♥   ♥

Treats in store!

Watch next month for the following absorbing stories:

AND DARE TO DREAM Elisabeth Scott
DRAGON LADY Stella Whitelaw
TROPICAL PARADISE Margaret Barker
COTTAGE HOSPITAL Margaret O'Neill

Available from Boots, Martins, John Menzies, W.H. Smith, Woolworths and other paperback stockists.

Also available from Mills and Boon Reader Service, P.O. Box 236, Thornton Road, Croydon, Surrey CR9 3RU.

Readers in South Africa — write to:
Independent Book Services Pty, Postbag X3010, Randburg, 2125, S. Africa.

Holiday
Survey 1991

At Mills & Boon we are keen to ensure that you can find our books whenever you want them, wherever you are - even when you are on holiday. Please spare a few minutes to fill in this questionnaire about your holidays and your reading habits, and we will send you a FREE book as our thank you.

1. How many holidays do you usually have a year?

a) In the U.K. _____ **b)** Abroad _____

2. When did you last have a holiday abroad?

Within the last 3 months ☐   2 to 5 years ago ☐

3 to 12 months ago ☐   More than 5 years ago ☐

1 to 2 years ago ☐   Never been on holiday abroad ☐

3. Which country did you last visit? _____

4. Do you usually buy Mills & Boon books when you are abroad?

Always ☐   Occasionally ☐

Once or twice ☐   Never ☐

5. How many Mills & Boon books did you buy on your last holiday abroad, and what series were they?

_____

6. Was there a good selection   Yes ☐   No ☐
of new titles available?

7. Where did you buy these books from?

Hotel ☐   Local Supermarket ☐

Foreign Airport ☐   Local Shops ☐

Beach Kiosk ☐   Holiday Complex ☐

Other (please specify) _____

8. How much did you pay for one Mills & Boon book?
(Approximate in pounds sterling £)

Up to £1.50 ☐   £1.51 to £2.00 ☐   £2.01 to £2.50 ☐

£2.51 to £3.00 ☐   More than £3.00 ☐

9. Did you consider this price to be:

Good value for money ☐   More expensive than expected ☐

Quite expensive, but worth it ☐   Very expensive ☐

10. If you did not buy a Mills & Boon book whilst on your holiday abroad why was this?

Could not find any ☐

Only found those I had already read ☐

Too expensive ☐

Took my own selection of holiday reading with me ☐

Other (please specify)_____

11. Do you buy any of the following when on holiday abroad? (Please state which ones).

British books (other than *Mills & Boon*)_____

British magazines_____

British newspapers_____

12. What age group are you?

16-24 ☐   25-34 ☐   35-44 ☐

45-54 ☐   55-64 ☐   65+ ☐

13. Are you working?

Full Time ☐   Part Time ☐   Not Working ☐

14. Are you a Mills & Boon Reader Service subscriber? Yes ☐ No ☐

THANK YOU FOR YOUR HELP

Please send to: **Mills & Boon Survey, P.O. Box 236, FREEPOST, Croydon, Surrey CR9 3EL**

Ms/Mrs/Miss/Mr_____ M&BE 3

Address_____

_____

_____

_____ Postcode_____

Offer expires December 31st 1991.The right is reserved to refuse an application and change the terms of this offer. Readers overseas and in Eire please send for details. Southern Africa write to Independent Book Services, Postbag X3010, Randburg 2125. You may be mailed with offers from other reputable companies as a result of this application. If you would prefer not to share in this opportunity please tick box ☐

mps
MAILING
PREFERENCE
SERVICE